A Cowboy's Heart:
Brie's Submission #11

By
Red Phoenix

* A portion of the story Includes the short "Stud Poker" part of the
retired anthology, *One Night in Vegas*. It is an important addition to
Master Anderson's journey.

Dedication

MrRed continues to inspire, and keeps me focused.
Life should be lived and enjoyed!

To my Master Brad Anderson fans...

You wanted to see more of him after reading about Amy & Troy,

so I added him to the staff of the Submissive Training Center.

You longed to know more about his story,

so I wrote this novel for you.

Much love!

~Red

All the peeps at Club Red
(a Red Phoenix club for fans by fans),
Thank you for your years of friendship, humor, and support.

CONTENTS

Secret

B rad Anderson was reluctant to leave Italy. It turned out that catching the garter belt had actually been a positive for him. He'd failed to understand until then just how alluring the idea of getting hitched was for a woman.

He'd been totally upfront with the ladies, making sure they understood he was headed back to the States as a single man. Brad planned to sample as many as he could in the short time he was there. However, one woman in particular, captured his attention—Julietta.

Julietta was an older woman with a magnetic smile and a free spirit. She'd pretty much claimed him during the reception, allowing the other girls to flirt but keeping his attention with her magical laughter and flirtatious grin.

The women who kept primping themselves while eying the competition couldn't hold his attention. He liked women who trusted in their natural beauty—like Julietta.

Brad had invited his newly formed harem onto the

dance floor, not wanting any to feel left out during the festive celebration. He *was* a gentleman at heart.

However, he did have an ulterior motive. Watching a woman dance gave him insight into the lady herself.

If she was awkward on the dance floor, you knew you had a woman who wasn't confident with her body, but might provide some entertainment and pleasure as you guided her to your needs—and hers.

A woman who was obvious in her sexual moves as she danced was letting the world know not only was she confident in her own skin, but she was hungry to devour her partner—or be devoured.

Some women were just pure energy, like the set of brown-eyed twins who had latched on to him. They were playful and fun on the dance floor, so full of vitality they were incapable of slowing down. It reminded him of a certain orange kitten he knew well.

Then there were women like Julietta. They danced with confidence but were subtle in their sexuality as they moved across the floor, elegant and graceful while maintaining an innocent flirtation that called to a man— inviting the chase. In the bedroom, it would translate into a charming power exchange.

Brad was definitely feeling her invitation and a few of the less couth women noticed. One, in particular, felt the need to state her dominance, wrapping her arms around his waist as she gyrated her body against his. While Brad didn't mind the act itself, it wasn't appropriate for a wedding. The last thing he needed was a raging boner on the dance floor.

With gentle hands, he pulled the young woman away,

twirling her once before letting go of her hand as he turned to face Julietta. He knew with certainty that she would keep it classy.

Brad smiled down at the woman, gratified to see the glint of mutual attraction reflected in her eyes. He gave each girl his attention that evening but kept coming back to the raven-haired beauty.

When the night began winding down, Brad offered his arm to her and asked Julietta to take a stroll in the garden.

"Isn't it too dark?" she asked in an enticing Italian accent.

"Absolutely not. You see, I know my way around the garden. I surveyed it early this morning. I'm certain I can guide you to the secret spot I found. Enchanting little place."

"You have me intrigued, *signore*."

He grinned. "As do you."

Brad put his hand on the small of her back, noting the way she subtly relaxed when he touched her. Another sign that she desired and invited this chase.

He was grateful for the soft moonlight as they strolled the maze of roses. Not too bright, but enough to aid him in navigating the labyrinth of foliage.

"How long do you plan to stay, *Signore* Anderson?"

"I actually will be heading out tomorrow. I have to finish packing for my move to LA, and still have a ton of loose ends to tie up with the school I'm headmaster of."

"School?" she asked with curiosity.

Now was the time to lay it all out there like a game of cards. She would either run away from him or right into his arms. Not one to back away from rejection, he answered, "Yes, I have a school for training Dominants and submissives."

The smirk on her face let him know she understood the curriculum involved.

"I take it you are familiar with those terms."

"Only in definition, *signore*," she replied coyly.

"I would be honored to give you a more in-depth lesson on the subject."

Julietta trilled with laughter but did not reply.

He let it go…for now, understanding the dance she'd begun. Too much interest shown on her part would make it seem the lady was desperate or uncouth. Therefore, it was his task to coax it from her like a gentleman, guiding her along with his subtle expertise until she could give in to her carnal desires.

Julietta was not a "wild one" but close enough to make her alluring to him.

He found the secluded spot he'd spied earlier in the day. It was bursting with colorful blooms, complete with a small water fountain and low marble bench.

She twirled in the center of the area with delight, reminding him of a young girl. "It is *magico*…" she cried.

"I quite agree," he answered, sitting down on the bench to admire her.

She stopped twirling and grinned at him, her eyebrows raised. "Do you take all your ladies here?"

He shook his head, a slow smile curving across his lips. "No, you are my first."

Julietta threw her hands up in joy and twirled some more.

He was already envisioning what he would do with her. A rose, a hard nipple, and love bite on the neck...

She stopped and sighed with contentment before walking toward him. Her hips swayed alluringly, calling to his masculine need.

Brad had learned from years of experience that it was important to let a woman know what to expect. He nonchalantly opened his legs a little wider, exposing the hardness of his cock outlined in his overly stretched pants.

Julietta instinctively glanced between his legs and her gaze remained frozen there.

A common reaction.

Either she would be up for the challenge of his large asset or she would make quick her escape. Better to know now.

"*Signore* Anderson, it appears you're happy to see me," she stated in amusement, looking him in the eye.

He responded in a low, seductive tone, "I am, Julietta."

Her eyes widened when he held out his hand to her.

"No reason to be scared. I aim to please," Brad assured her when the woman didn't move.

"Hmm..." she murmured, her eyes transfixed on his massive shaft.

"Curious what it would feel like buried inside you?"

Julietta gasped, her chest rising and falling quickly.

His grin was wicked when he added, "I'm sure we would be a good fit."

She met his gaze, licking her lips nervously. Brad felt certain she was interested in testing out his theory, but what he needed to do now was romance the lady so she would be prepared for the challenge of his sizeable cock.

He patted the bench. "Why don't you sit while I pick a rose to seduce you with?"

Julietta giggled as she took a seat on the marble bench.

Brad stood up, walked over to a large rosebush, and pulled the stem of a red blossom toward him. "Are you a red rose?" he asked, taking a whiff of the flower. He looked at her, shaking his head. "No." He released the bloom and it snapped back into place.

He moved to the next bush covered in yellow roses. Grasping the large round head of the rose, he leaned over and took in its scent. "Too sweet," he commented, letting it go.

The next bush was bursting with lavender flowers, which also sported thin, spiky thorns. "A pleasant fragrance, but a little too vicious for you."

He walked over to the other side and took hold of a cream-colored rose lined with a blush of pink edges. Taking a long inhale, he sighed in appreciation. "Yes, this is you, Julietta. The rose smells of fruit and spice."

He broke the long stem and walked back to her, lowering the rose for her to smell.

She took in its scent and moaned softly. "Perfection."

"Like you," he agreed, sitting down beside her. "Will you permit me to seduce you with this worthy blossom?"

She smiled. "How to you propose to do that, *signore?*"

"It will require you to undress."

Julietta laughed, looking around anxiously.

"No need to fear. No one will find us here," he said confidently as he started unbuttoning his jacket. "To put you at ease, I will be the first to undress."

She watched in rapt attention as he removed his jacket, vest, and tie before unbuttoning his white shirt. Brad heard her barely audible sigh when he shrugged it off, exposing his muscular chest.

A smile played at her lips as she tried unsuccessfully not to stare. A refined lady…

He moved in closer and offered, "Can I assist you?"

She only nodded, holding her breath when he began unbuttoning her silk blouse, pulling it down over her shoulder to expose a sexy lace bra that complemented the pearls around her neck.

"May I?" he asked, looking pointedly at her brassiere.

"Please, *signore*," she replied, a little breathless. Despite the dim lighting, Brad could swear the mature beauty was blushing.

He reached behind her, consciously letting his skin barely brush against hers. She gasped again when he unclasped the bra and eased it from her shoulders.

There Julietta was in all her naked beauty, her feminine features enhanced by the pale moonlight. As much as he desired to suckle those fabulous breasts, Brad asked her to turn from him and lean against his torso.

His request must have surprised her based on her shocked expression, but she did as he asked, tentatively reclining against his bare chest.

"There now, doesn't that feel more comfortable?"

"*Sì*," she whispered softly.

Brad wrapped one arm around her waist as he began teasing her skin with the soft petals of the rose. Goosebumps rose on her skin as he glided the flower over her arm to her stomach and then up to the curvature of her breasts. He then stroked her long neck with it and heard her moan softly.

His cock responded to the sound of her pleasure, hardening against the small of her back. There was no hiding his body's reaction, nor the size of his excitement.

"Do you like the caress of the rose, Julietta?" he growled into her ear.

"I do, *Signore* Anderson."

He grinned when he instructed her, "You may call me *Padrone*."

She stiffened as she turned her head toward him. "Master?"

Brad answered confidently, "*Si.*"

Julietta settled back in his embrace, a little tenser, but with a definite smile on her lips.

"Do you mind if I go a little lower?" he asked.

"Not at all, *Padrone*."

He found the title arousing when it was spoken with her alluring accent. He set down the rose and tugged on the side zipper of her skirt. He slipped his hands underneath the material and eased it down just below her hips, exposing simple white cotton panties.

To him, they were the little black dress of the panty world—always in style and always flattering on a woman.

"Shimmy out of that skirt, Julietta. I want full access to explore you." He pressed her against him so she would feel the stiffness of his cock.

Julietta did as she was told, but she was slow to respond and he heard the increase in her breath as she lay back against him. He knew she was both turned-on and slightly frightened by what was about to happen.

Both reactions pleased him.

Brad ran the flower down her stomach and lightly grazed her covered mound. Julietta leaned back harder against him as she opened her legs. Both were indications that she was desirous for his intimate caress.

"If I were to touch your pussy, would I find it wet?" he growled into her ear.

She giggled softly.

"I take that as a yes, but must discover for myself." He glided his fingers down to her mound and groaned when he felt how soaked her panties were. "Julietta, it appears you are happy to see me."

Her low laughter increased his libido. Brad appreciated a woman who knew what she wanted but allowed the man to lead the seduction. He was certain she would make a pleasing submissive.

Brad returned his attention to her breasts, concentrating on tickling her erect nipples while he snuck a hand down to slip under the thin material of her panties. Julietta froze in his arms but did not resist as he slid his finger over her wet clit. She was very slippery, the kind of slickness that would allow for a spirited coupling.

Keeping his finger resting against her clit, he brought the rose to her lips. "Do you know what the name of this rose is?"

She shook her head, smiling at him flirtatiously.

He whispered in her ear, "Secret."

9

"Really, *signore*?" she scoffed.

"I would never lie to a lady," he assured her.

Julietta took the rose from him, admiring it before putting it to her nose to sniff it again. "I love this flower."

"Of course you do. The flower *is* you, and 'secret' would be a good pet name."

She smiled, blushing when she told him, "For a big bad *Padrone*, you seem awfully sweet."

"Who says a Master can't romance his partner's mind before he dominates her body?"

Julietta tilted her head in reflective thought. "Are flowers your tool of choice then, *signore*?"

"I prefer the bullwhip."

Brad heard her sharp intake of breath, and enjoyed watching her swallow down her fear. He pulled back her hair and nuzzled her neck, explaining, "I like to tie my women up, vulnerable and naked, so I can show them the many characteristics of my whip. I want them to feel both the pleasure and pain I can cause."

Julietta let out a soft whimper.

"I have the power to lightly lick your skin with my whip or take your breath away with its hard slash."

He felt her tremble in his arms.

"Tonight, however, we will simply challenge your pussy with my cock."

She moaned, turning toward him for a kiss. Brad fisted her hair and thrust his tongue inside her mouth, aching to feel the tight confines of her pussy.

"*Padrone*..."

He pulled at her panties. "Yes, secret?"

"Please…" she whispered lustfully.

He removed her panties and asked her to stand before him as he slowly undressed. There was always the chance she would balk when he revealed his naked cock for the first time. Brad watched her eyes as he unzipped his pants and lowered both his briefs and slacks—his shaft standing proud and ready before her.

Julietta's lips trembled as she stared at it.

He kicked his pants away and smirked. "Are you ready to test your limits?"

She nodded.

Brad lay on his back on the cold marble bench, his manhood standing straight and tall. "Come here and lower yourself onto me. Let's find out how much of my cock you can take."

Julietta approached him, a coy smile on her lips. He was grateful she appreciated a good challenge.

Helping her to straddle him, Brad grasped his shaft and held it still as she rubbed her soft folds against it.

"That's right. Get it thoroughly wet with your excitement. It'll make it easier for me to pound you."

Her eyes lit up at the mention of pounding, and she smiled at him as she pushed her opening against the head of his massive cock.

"Bounce against it."

Julietta began bouncing up and down, her tight pussy resistant to the girth of his shaft. But the woman was not deterred and continued to rub and press herself against it until she succeeded in taking the head of his shaft.

When it slipped inside, Brad groaned deeply, closing his eyes to savor the caress of her strong inner muscles.

Julietta began grunting and crying out as she tried to take more of his length. He put his hands on her waist to help, but consciously chose not to force her to take more than she could handle.

He could seriously hurt a woman if he wasn't careful.

After several minutes of focused attempts, she looked down at him and sighed. His cock was buried halfway into her mound, and that appeared to be all her body could take. Knowing what he had to work with, Brad made a mental note of the depth before he took control and began moving her up and down his branch of a shaft.

Julietta threw her head back and cried out loudly.

He chuckled. "Shhh… We don't want people following your cries of passion."

She bit her lip but kept her head back as he gave her what she could handle. Experience had taught him that few could take his full length, and body type was no indicator—young Brie had been a prime example and a welcomed surprise. Normally he concentrated on the intense stimulation around the head of his cock rather than lament at the lack of depth.

Julietta continued to cry out and groan as she bounced enthusiastically on his shaft. He could have come right then and there, but he needed to dominate her hot pussy so he lifted her off him.

She looked shocked and bereft until he patted the bench, telling her to get on her hands and knees.

Julietta climbed onto it and looked behind her, her eyes widened in fear as he approached with his raging hard-on to position himself. "Relax," he told her soothingly as he placed one hand on her shapely ass. "I'm in control now."

She moaned when he pressed his cock against her and forced his way in.

"Rock against me and show me how deep you can take it."

She began a seductive rocking motion while Master Anderson looked down and observed his cock disappearing inside her depths. When she made no more progress, he grabbed her hips.

"Now that you have fucked my cock, I am going to pound that hot pussy of yours."

Julietta whimpered in anticipation, tensing as she readied herself for the onslaught.

"Relax," he reminded her again. "Give in to *my* need." Julietta moaned as he grasped her waist. Brad gritted his teeth as he pounded her, concentrating hard on keeping each stroke the same depth.

"*Padrone…Padrone…*" she cried out in unrestrained passion.

The sexiness of her voice and her wet, willing body proved to be too much. Brad stilled, digging his fingers into her flesh as he blessed her with a massive come. His lustful groan filled the night air, and then there was silence.

Julietta collapsed onto the stone bench when he pulled out. He lay on top of her, partially supporting his weight with his limbs.

"Secret," he whispered huskily into her ear.

"*Si, Padrone*, I am your secret," she agreed softly.

He pressed against her more forcefully, kissing the

back of her neck before latching his lips and teeth to her tender skin. He rubbed her clit, bringing her to orgasm as he sucked hard.

Julietta cried out in surprise and then purred as the pleasure washed over her. Brad pulled away, satisfied by the mark he'd left. Invisible to others when covered by her hair, but a physical reminder to her of their night together.

"If you ever find yourself in California, I'd be happy to treat you to a session with my bullwhip."

Julietta said nothing, but he felt her shiver—whether from the night air, the aftereffects of their inspired fucking, or the mention of the bullwhip, he was unsure.

Brad stood up, picking the flower off the ground and breaking the stem closer to the head of the blossom. When Julietta stood beside him, he tucked it behind her ear and smiled down at her. "My secret."

"Thank you, *Padrone*."

He brushed her cheek lightly before gathering her clothes and helping Julietta into them.

After donning his own, he guided her out of the dark garden and kissed her good night.

"I will consider your invitation," she murmured, touching the rose in her hair as she left his side.

Brad watched her walk up the stairs of the castle, swaying her hips seductively. She was a special woman, he mused, a true gift to remember Italy by.

He headed up to his bedroom, exhausted but satisfied, and was surprised to find the twins waiting patiently at his door.

"*Signore* Anderson, you've returned!" they squealed in

unison.

He shook his head, chuckling as he unlocked his door. "Would you ladies like a nightcap?"

"*Per favore!*"

Changes

It was a long plane ride home, but Brad used it to organize his list. He was concerned about selling his Denver home. There simply wasn't enough time for him to do it himself, and the housing market had been in a slump recently. To sell now would mean losing money, and as a businessman, he found that thought goaded him to no end. He'd simply have to come up with another solution that didn't involve renters. God only knew what they would do to his pristine place.

As far as The Denver Academy, it was harder to give up control of her than he'd thought it would be. Yes, he still had ownership, but someone *else* would be taking the reins. He was grateful Samantha was staying behind to oversee the transition. The Domme had years of experience as a trainer at the LA Submissive Training Center, and knew firsthand the high standards required.

However, The Academy represented his dreams. Brad had worked hard his entire life to create it. The school was his baby and now it felt like he was abandoning her.

Brad shifted in his seat.

Oh hell, why am I getting all sentimental? Shit, man, it's just a business investment.

He closed his computer and turned off the overhead light. He needed to rest, that's all. Closing his eyes, he groaned inwardly when the infant in the seat behind him started crying.

Children were such an unwanted nuisance. Why were they even allowed on planes?

Brad grabbed his headphones and turned the volume up. Forcing his eyes closed again, he took several deep breaths. With determination he finally drifted off to sleep.

There she was…standing at the top of the hill facing toward the mountains. Brad reached out to her.

"Amy."

She didn't respond to his voice, so he moved closer, calling her name again.

The beautiful redhead continued to stare ahead without acknowledging him. He had a choice; he knew it in the core of his being.

It was now or never—he could walk away or fight for her love.

He wasn't willing to lose her again.

"Amy! Turn around and face me."

The redhead moved her head slightly in response to his voice, but stayed rooted where she was.

He felt the heartbreak all over again. The shock of watching her walk away from him into the arms of another. His voice broke when he called out to her, "Don't, Amy, don't let this chance fade away. This is *our* chance at happiness."

The redhead looked at her wrist and then to the left, as if she were expecting someone.

"I deserve to be happy," he stated firmly.

The redhead lowered her head in sorrow as if she'd finally heard him.

"We can forget about the past. It's about you and me now."

He saw her shoulders tense as she lifted her head, taking one last look to the left before turning toward him, her lovely hair blowing in the breeze and covering her face. Amy had finally chosen him.

The intense love he felt threatened to unravel his very being. "Damn it, Amy. I love you, I always have…"

The redhead moved the hair from her face and gazed up at him.

His eyes were blinded by a flash of brilliant light shining from her and he was swallowed whole.

Brad jumped in his seat, not only waking himself but also startling the old woman beside him.

"It's all right, ma'am," he apologized. "Just woke myself up from a dream is all."

The elderly lady was dressed in a housecoat, similar to what his grandmother used to wear. She patted his arm, smiling when she asked, "Good dream or bad?"

He thought back on it, and shook his head. The thrill of finally winning Amy's heart still reverberated inside his very soul, even though he knew it hadn't been real. He smiled down when he answered, "I'm not sure, really."

"Assume it was good then," she advised.

Brad nodded, lying back against the headrest and closing his eyes. The baby started crying again behind him, and he sighed in disgust.

Amy had a child now. There was no turning back. He needed to leave Denver or forever be haunted by a love that could never be returned.

One good thing came from that long plane trip. Brad had gotten up to stretch his legs and noticed a man who looked an awful lot like Nosaka. Seeing the man started Brad down a line of thought that eventually put a smile on his face.

One problem solved, he said to himself, gloating as he walked off the plane.

He called Samantha first and asked her to meet at his house early the next day.

Coming home, he was greeted by a very unhappy kitten. Cayenne purposely avoided him, hiding out under various pieces of furniture and eyeing him accusingly.

"You can pout all you want, little lady, but I know you want me to scratch your chin."

The orange tabby gave him a pitiful meow.

Brad got onto the floor and held out his arms to her. "Stop being so stubborn. I had to leave. If I could have brought you, I would have."

She was not moved by his speech, and slunk under the coffee table, turning her back on him.

"Really, such behavior is unbecoming, Cayenne."

Brad chuckled, admiring her obstinance. He knew how much she longed to be caressed but she was determined to punish him, and wasn't giving an inch.

Brad got up from the floor and rifled through his carry-on, producing a carefully wrapped plant. He freed it from the plastic and held it up to admire. The green plant was housed in an elaborately painted terra-cotta pot. "I want you to know that I got hassled by customs bringing you this treat. But when I saw it I thought of you and couldn't resist." He set the potted plant on the floor and waited patiently.

Cayenne stared at the plant, her tail swinging back and forth. He knew she could smell its alluring scent, and she crept a little closer.

"That's it, little lady."

She glanced up at him with those green eyes and mewed.

Brad smiled. "Forgiven?"

She cautiously took another step forward and then another as she approached the plant. Cayenne took a sniff and sat down, grabbing the plant with her forepaws in a cat hug as she rubbed her face in the leaves—now oblivious of him.

"So that's how it is. You just want me for my cat-nip."

Cayenne's eyes grew wide and her tail started twitching crazily. Suddenly, she jumped straight up in the air and took off running, sliding on the wood floors and into a wall. She ran around the room jumping on one piece of furniture before springing off to tackle another—the small kitten making a complete fool of herself.

Brad watched with amusement. After several minutes, Cayenne calmed down and began to meow as she walked toward him. He held out his arms again, and the tabby climbed up them and onto his shoulder.

He scratched under her chin, and the kitten began to purr.

"Are we square then?"

She rubbed her cheek against his chin, claiming him with her scent.

"I'll take that as a yes."

Brad answered the door, pleased that Samantha was even earlier than expected because he had a full day ahead, but stopped short as soon as he saw what she was wearing.

"What the hell do you have on?" he complained, looking at her business suit and tall, sexy heels.

She frowned. "This is what I normally wear to a meeting."

"Well, I sure hope you can pack in those clothes, Samantha, because we're going to work while I discuss my plans."

Undeterred, she undid her jacket and placed it over a chair. Kicking off her heels, she placed them underneath. She then rolled up her sleeves and faced him with a superior grin. "Not a problem."

Brad nodded in approval. "You look good barefoot. Feel free to take off your clothes if you get uncomfortable."

With that he pulled off his T-shirt and flexed his pecs for her.

Samantha raised an eyebrow. "Are you propositioning me, Master Anderson? I have my cane in the car."

He chuckled. "Ah, Samantha, I like your sense of humor. Make no mistake, it would be *I* who would be caning you."

Samantha snorted. "In your dreams…"

Cayenne made her appearance, strolling leisurely from Brad's bedroom and jumping up the arm he offered to settle on his shoulder. She stared at Samantha intensely.

"How did you two get along?" Brad asked.

"She hid the whole damn time. Never saw the cat, but the bowl was always empty and the cat box needed cleaning daily."

Brad turned toward Cayenne. "You should thank Samantha, little lady. She's the only reason you had food and water while I was gone."

Cayenne touched his cheek with her cold little nose and then rubbed her furry face against his jaw.

"She was miffed at me for leaving her and took it out on you, I'm afraid," he apologized.

"Like I care what the cat does."

Brad grinned, scratching the feline's tiny head. "You should, Samantha. Animals can teach us a lot."

Samantha shook her head. "Oh, like your claims that talking to plants is a healthy habit?"

"It is," he insisted. "If humans interacted with plants and animals on a regular basis, the whole world would be a better place. We're all connected you know."

"Says Farmer Joe from Hicktown," Samantha teased. She glanced around the room. "So where do I start and what did you have me come here to discuss?"

"Before we begin, I must give you this." Brad handed her a red box with a shiny gold bow.

"You didn't have to," she insisted.

"It's a simple thank you gift."

Samantha huffed. "Totally unnecessary…" but Brad didn't miss the slight upturn of her blood-red lips when she untied the bow. Her eyes lit up when she carefully lifted the sleek figurine of a golden glass cat. Stripes of intricate colors highlighted the breathtaking piece of art.

"A little something to remind you of Cayenne and me."

"It's truly exquisite," Samantha exclaimed in awe as she slowly turned the figurine to admire every angle.

"Authentic Venetian glass made by an old man with withered hands that move like an angel's when he creates."

Samantha carefully put the glass cat back in its box and took a moment before she spoke. "Thank you for this…"

He put one arm around her, squeezing tight when she tried to pull away. "Ah, it's nothing. Just wanted to say thanks. Not just for taking care of my little girl, but for handling the transition of The Academy for me."

She looked up at him, squirming uncomfortably in his embrace. "Think nothing of it, Master Anderson."

"I'm serious, Samantha. Knowing you're looking out for my investment means a lot to me."

She shrugged off his arm and turned to face him.

"Look, you gave me a second chance after The Submissive Training Center fired me. I owe you for that."

"Being equally frank here, it benefitted us both. I respect your skills as a Domme, as well as your uncompromising focus."

She smiled briefly. "Although I was initially resistant to your comical antics, you managed to run a first-class school here. The businessman in you shines through, even if there's a prank waiting around the corner at any moment."

"Life without laughter is boring. I don't recommend it."

Samantha's expression suddenly changed, becoming serious. "How is Thane? Did the wedding go off without a hitch?"

"Oh, you know Thane…" He laughed. "Everything was perfect, including the bride."

She nodded, looking off in the distance. "Brianna has proven herself to be an adequate submissive."

He smirked. "Adequate?"

"Thane deserves only the best. It is good that he seems satisfied."

"I'd say he's more than satisfied. He was rutting after the poor girl the entire reception. You'd have thought by the way he was acting that they'd never fucked before."

She shook her head, laughing. "He's always had a healthy appetite. So…what about Durov?"

She tried to pass the question off nonchalantly, but Brad faced her square on, knowing it was a touchy subject for the Domme. "What exactly do you want to know?"

Samantha was slow to answer. "Does he...seem happy? Has he collared a submissive yet?"

"The man has many collared submissives, Samantha."

"But...has he found the one?"

Brad folded his arms. "Why are you asking?"

Samantha turned away from him when she said, "I need to know Rytsar is happy. It would help give me closure."

"Durov had a grand time at the reception if that's what you mean. No reason to concern yourself further about his well-being."

She nodded curtly, quickly changing the subject. "So what's the reason for this meeting, besides free labor?"

Brad winked at her, handing Samantha a box and packing paper. He pointed to his mantel above the fireplace. It wasn't until they got themselves settled and working that he told her. "I've decided not to give this place up."

Samantha stopped packing and stared at him, her mouth slack. "You're not moving? Is all of this just another elaborate joke of yours?"

"Now wouldn't that be funny," he said with a chuckle. "No, I'm still headed to LA but I'm not selling this house. I've decided to ask Nosaka to be the caretaker. He's the only man I know who will treat this house *and* my garden with the nurturing they need."

"Why tell me?" the Domme mumbled as she took a knickknack from the mantel and quickly wrapped it in protective paper.

"I'm also going to have him visit The Academy from

time to time."

Samantha set the item in the box slowly, eyeing him with suspicion. "Why?"

"To be your backup. I suspect you may experience some flack from the new management, and you'll need a second opinion."

"I don't need anyone," she spat.

Brad shook his head. "Yes, you do. This transition isn't a one-man job, Samantha. I'm sure you'll agree that Nosaka has the ability to calm ruffled feathers. He makes the perfect negotiator when things get dicey."

"I don't like having a man usurp my power," she growled, grabbing another knickknack from the mantel and wrapping it in paper angrily.

"Samantha, you're going to have to play nice with the new staff. Give them the benefit of the doubt, but if there's ever a time you don't see eye to eye, send Nosaka in to settle the matter amicably."

"So Nosaka's my babysitter?"

Brad's nostrils flared. "No, Samantha. Nosaka's formal role will be to oversee the financial success of *my* business. However, if you should have need, he will be there to support you as well."

"I doubt very much I will ever have to use him."

"As do I," Brad agreed, grabbing his own box to start on the bookcase.

He suspected Samantha would work exceedingly hard with the new staff to make it a smooth transition without any help from Nosaka—which was exactly what Brad intended.

Good-bye

With a heavy heart, Brad threw the last of his belongings in the back of his Chevy truck and tied them down. He looked back at his house, knowing with certainty he would not be coming back.

He noticed movement in his neighbor's window and smiled.

A feeling of nostalgia came over him, and he beckoned Courtney to come out to join him. The woman stood frozen in the frame of the window and then pointed to herself with a look of disbelief.

Brad nodded in affirmation.

He noticed it took Courtney several minutes to appear. Her makeup had been hastily done, and she smelled of overbearing perfume that preceded her as she approached him.

"So you're really leaving, huh?"

He frowned slightly. "Afraid so, Ms. Courtney."

"Are you coming back?"

"No."

Her shoulders slumped. "Do you know who's moving in?"

"I do."

She shot Brad a look of concern when he didn't immediately answer. "Please don't tell me it's a family with screaming kids."

He smiled down at her, shaking his head. "I would never be so cruel."

"Who then?"

"A distinguished gentleman who follows the black arts. Whatever you do, Courtney, don't upset the man. I've seen firsthand what can happen when someone steps on his chi."

"Chi?"

"Yeah, it's some mysterious Asian thing. You don't want to mess with the chi."

Courtney looked legitimately frightened. "How do I avoid upsetting his chi?"

"Never look him in the eye, even if he speaks to you. Keep your head bowed and your hands together in a prayer of protection. He'll respect the prayer and won't call on his powers. But, Courtney, if he *ever* catches you spying on him, he'll call down his dark arts."

Her eyes widened when he explained, "It will be subtle at first. A little hair loss, a rash that won't go away...but it'll get worse. Much worse."

She shuddered. "I'd rather take the screaming kids."

"I didn't have a choice. I owed the man."

"You *know* him?"

Brad nodded his head solemnly.

"How?"

"I can't say."

Courtney let out a nervous sigh.

Brad put his hand on her shoulder. "Don't worry. He's a good man if you keep your distance." Her body trembled under his hand. He wasn't sure if it was out of fear or sexual desire—but he suspected both.

"Promise you'll do that for me."

"I will," she vowed.

Brad put his finger under her chin and tilted her head up to look her in the eye. "Shall we seal that promise with a kiss?"

She froze like a statue when he leaned down. He wanted to formally seal the deal so Nosaka would not be harassed. It was the least he could do, so he gave Courtney a long, deep, satisfying kiss.

The woman wobbled on her feet when he let go.

"If I come back to Denver to visit, I don't want to find you bald, blotchy, and toothless."

She only nodded, unable to speak.

Brad opened the door of his truck and grabbed his black Stetson, placing it on his head. Now that he was leaving Colorado for good, he decided to fully embrace his cowboy heritage. "I guess this is it for this cowboy."

Courtney waved good-bye to him, a dreamy look on her face.

Brad shut the door and huffed as he buckled up. Giving Cayenne a pat on the head, he grumbled, "I hate good-byes."

She proceeded to climb onto his lap and purr.

Brad hit the gas and sped down the road, looking back in the rearview mirror one last time at his mountain home in the suburbs.

Good-bye, Amy…

Brad pulled up to the luxurious Nyte Hotel and let out a long, exhausted sigh.

Damn, I need this.

An energetic young man hustled up to the massive vehicle with a friendly grin and opened his door. "Nice truck, sir. We don't get many of those here."

Brad glanced around, noting the abundance of sleek sports cars and convertibles. He shrugged as he picked up the mewing orange tabby from the seat, cradling the kitten in his muscular arms as he petted her under the chin.

"Yeah, well, I'm not from around here…"

"So where *do* you call home?"

Although the young man was being overly social, Brad answered the question. "Denver, but I'm headed to LA to stake my claim."

The kid laughed good-naturedly, glancing at his cowboy hat. "Mister, I hate to break it to you, but you're going to stick out like a sore thumb there, too." He quickly added, "Not that there's anything wrong with that."

Brad pulled out a small leather bag and gently eased the kitten into it, zipping the tiny animal inside. He put a finger to his lips, knowing pets were not allowed at the posh hotel. He handed the valet a twenty and explained, "After all the upheaval of packing, the only thing I'm interested in tonight is a relaxing evening before I head off to LA tomorrow."

"You're only here for a night, sir?"

Brad mirrored the boy's engaging smile. "That's all the time I could spare. You see, I'm the new headmaster of the Training Center, and the next session starts in a week."

"What kind of training—if you don't mind me asking?"

Brad chuckled as he shook his finger at the valet. "It's the kind of training that would get a young man like you in trouble." Picking up a small suitcase from the back, Brad handed over the keys.

As he started toward the hotel entrance, the valet called out, "Sir."

Brad turned around and raised an eyebrow. "Yes?"

With a wicked grin, the boy waved the keys in the air. "Is it true what they say about men and big trucks?"

Brad smiled, amused by his cheekiness. "What? You mean 'Big truck, big...heart'?"

The valet nodded, laughing to himself as he jumped into the beast of a machine. The deep rumble of the engine reverberated in the courtyard as he drove off.

Brad lifted the leather bag level with his face and whispered, "Keep silent, Cayenne. They welcome pussies here, but not ones of the feline persuasion."

He entered the revolving door of the hotel and looked over the foyer with satisfaction. The huge crystal chandelier hanging from the ceiling was impressive, along with the marble pillars that surrounded it. The entire lobby was adorned with lavish amounts of silver and gold.

Mr. Nyte certainly had a flair for the dramatic.

The hotel was known worldwide as an elite establishment, famous for its high-stakes poker and deluxe fantasy suites. It was funny that Brad was only interested in a comfortable bed and a relaxing evening to himself.

A sexy brunette sauntered past, looking him over favorably. She glanced down at his crotch and let out a little purr of approval. "Howdy, cowboy."

Master Anderson smirked as he tipped his hat to her. "Ma'am."

When she proceeded to bite her lip in an inviting manner, Brad abruptly broke eye contact and headed toward the front desk.

Rest and relaxation, he cautioned himself.

The perky young woman at the front desk typed in his information and smiled sweetly as she confirmed, "I see you have a reservation for the Serenity Suite for one night. Is that correct, Mr. Anderson?"

"It is, but I want to confirm that I won't be disturbed by the chaos of your casino." As if on cue, there was a loud outburst of bells just beyond the foyer; the sound of cheering soon followed.

She grinned, announcing proudly, "Must be another big winner."

"My point exactly."

"Rest assured, Mr. Anderson. The Serenity Suite is specially designed to meet your nee—" The girl made a cute little sneeze sound and blushed, looking quite embarrassed. "Pardon me." She discreetly wiped her nose with a tissue before continuing. "The walls are insulated with special material so they are completely soundproof. The only sounds you'll hear are the ones you make yourself."

"That's good to know," he replied, winking at her as the crowd in the casino broke out in a fresh set of cheers.

"If you'll just..." The young woman sneezed again, looking mortified. "I'm so sorry. If you could just put your thumb there for me, you'll be all set." She pointed to a small scanner and smiled.

Brad quickly placed his thumb on the device to let it scan his fingerprint, hoping Cayenne would remain quiet a little longer.

"Will there be anything else, sir?"

"Nope...wait. Can I schedule a massage?"

"Why, of course." Her face lit up as she explained, "I'd be happy to send one of our massage therapists up to your room. Would you like a male or female to attend to you?"

Brad shook his head. "No, no... I'm not wanting a private session. I'd prefer the spa and *no* women present."

The young woman sneezed again, blushing a deeper shade of red. "I truly apologize..." She turned away from him to wipe her nose again. "Let me get our concierge, Francesca Young. I'm positive she can set something up for you."

Brad glanced down at the moving bag on the counter. "That's okay. Just have her call my room."

"Oh, it's no trouble, Mr. Anderson," a confident female voice stated behind him.

He turned to see a slender woman with soft brown eyes and a stunning smile. "I live to accommodate our guests."

She grabbed the bag on the counter with a knowing smile. "I'm Francesca, and I'd be happy to escort you to your room while we discuss your *unique* needs on the way up."

Brad chuckled, knowing he'd been caught. "Why the hell not, Francesca?"

As the elevator doors closed she opened the bag, and Cayenne's head popped out. "Well now, aren't you a little cutie?"

She petted the top of the kitten's head but gave Brad a stern look, stating, "The Nyte doesn't allow pets in our fantasy suites, Mr. Anderson."

"I was aware," he conceded, "and I agree allergies are nothing to sneeze at. However, Cayenne isn't a pet." He scratched the bottom of the kitten's chin, causing her to purr. "This is my companion."

Francesca gave a curt nod. "I have cats of my own and understand, Mr. Anderson. It is an honor to have you join us tonight so you may keep your companion, and I will see to it that the room is thoroughly cleaned after your departure. Do you need one of my staff to fetch cat sand for her?"

"Nope, it's already taken care of. You are very kind, Miss Young."

She smiled graciously. "About the massage you requested…we do have private rooms at the spa. I'd be happy to arrange a session with our finest masseuse."

"A man, please. I do *not* need the distraction of female hands on me tonight." Just the mere thought of it had his shaft hardening. He nonchalantly moved his suitcase to cover the growing bulge.

"Certainly. Carl is the best we have, and I assure you he'll have no interest in your assets, Mr. Anderson," Francesca said in a businesslike tone as she glanced away, a smile playing on her lips.

Brad laughed to himself, only slightly embarrassed. As they exited the elevator, he asked her, "What time should I come down to the spa?"

Francesca checked the schedule on her phone and announced, "It looks like Carl has an opening in two hours. Will that work for you, Mr. Anderson?"

"Suits me just fine." Brad placed his thumb on the keypad, and the doors slowly swung open, revealing an impressive living area with a killer view of the city.

The sound of a waterfall caught his attention. He looked to his left and saw a glass wall with cascading electric blue water. In the center of the unusual wall was a gold-framed doorway that led into an elegant dining room.

"Very nice," he complimented.

"In the bedroom you will find a full-size recessed hot tub as well as a walk-in shower for two that includes the added feature of music and custom lighting."

"It seems you've thought of everything."

"We want our clients to be fully satisfied."

"Well, there's no question I will be sleeping like a baby tonight."

"That reminds me," she stated, "the bed has the world's top-rated mattress. If you do not feel it is the best sleep you've ever had, please let me know."

"I'll do that," he promised. As she was turning to leave, Brad reached out and touched her lightly on the shoulder. A blush rose to her cheeks from the simple contact. "I appreciate you taking care of the Cayenne situation, Miss Young."

"It's my pleasure, Mr. Anderson. Don't hesitate to call me if you require anything else. It's my sincere and distinct honor to serve the new headmaster of The Submissive Training Center. Many of your graduates end up visiting us and have only praise for what you do there."

"Just how many people know I'm here?" Brad asked, suddenly concerned that his privacy might be compromised.

"Only the essential staff. We respect your need for anonymity," Francesca replied with a charming smile as she shut the double doors behind her.

He felt rather foolish not anticipating the far-reaching consequences of becoming the headmaster of LA's renowned Training Center. Before, Brad had never considered what it was like to represent the school 24/7, no matter where he was. He found it disquieting, and now had more sympathy for his friend Thane Davis, who'd been headmaster of the school for years.

More than ever, he *needed* this night of relaxation. Once he hit LA, his life would no longer be his. Cradling Cayenne in his arms, he gently stroked her while staring out over the brightly lit city. "It appears our life is about to change in ways I wasn't expecting, girl. I already miss Denver."

She mewed softly, rubbing her cheek against his hand. Brad looked down at the kitten and felt a brief moment of heartache.

Shey Allen

B rad shared a quick snack of canned tuna fish with
Cayenne before heading down to the spa. He
spooned another bite for her and watched with satisfaction as she gobbled it up. "Hungry, are you?"

She looked up at him expectantly as he was about to
take his own bite. He chuckled, then gave her his
portion. "Well, a growing girl needs to eat." He petted
her back and was rewarded with her little body vibrating
in a happy purr.

Once she finished the can, he tossed it in the trash
and took a quick shower in the fancy bathroom. He
played with the dials until he found a soothing station,
then adjusted the lighting to alternate between blue,
yellow, and green, in time with the music. The shower-
head was massive and rained down warm water over his
tired muscles.

Even the soap had a relaxing scent, adding to the
whole "serenity" vibe.

It made him wonder: if Mr. Nyte had perfected a serenity room, what the hell was the BDSM suite like? He

decided it might warrant a trip back to the hotel to find out.

Brad dressed in simple sweats and a thin T-shirt, pulling the brim of his cowboy hat down to avoid being recognized before he headed out. He was already feeling much more relaxed after his shower and knew sleep would come easily after a deep-tissue massage.

The stress of packing his home and transferring power over to the new staff of his Denver Academy had taken a toll on his body. Hell, he was stiff in places he never knew existed before—and that was saying a lot.

A session with his bullwhip would have helped tremendously because he found the power exchange relaxing to his soul. However, he hadn't had time for that before leaving Denver, and had decided to wait until he was settled in his new position before he sought a partner to play with.

Brad entered the spa, lowering his head when he spied the herd of scantily clad women in short silk robes running about.

Damn, women were beautiful creatures...

He quickly made his way to the front desk to avoid contact with any of them. "I have an appointment with Carl."

"And your name, sir?"

Brad looked up and found himself momentarily speechless, stunned by the beautiful redhead who stood before him. Seeing her reminded him of Amy, and the wound that he'd so carefully tended was unceremoniously ripped back open.

The girl smiled pleasantly, unaware of the pain she'd

just inflicted on him.

"Name's Anderson. Brad Anderson," he mumbled. He turned away from her as he leaned against the desk, trying to appear casual when he was anything but.

"Welcome, Mr. Anderson. I know Miss Young penciled you in, but I'm sorry to inform you that Carl is running a few minutes late. Will that be a problem for you?"

Brad shook his head, unwilling to brave another look at her. "As long as it's only a few minutes, I'm fine."

He tensed when he felt her hand on his shoulder a few seconds later. Her light touch stirred him in ways he hadn't expected, and didn't want.

"I've brought you some water. It always pays to stay hydrated in Vegas," she advised him with an endearing smile—her blue eyes drawing him in with their gentle sincerity. A light rose-colored blush covered her cheeks when their eyes met. She quickly lowered her gaze, but the damage was already done.

Oh God…there was nothing sexier than a redhead's blush.

"Thank you," he replied gruffly, taking it from her and immediately unscrewing the lid to take a swig, wanting to avoid any further contact.

The girl was absolutely exquisite: long red hair framed an angel-like face, giving her an innocent look that those big blue eyes only accentuated.

She whispered under her breath so no one else would hear, "I respect what you do, Mr. Anderson."

He glanced at her sideways. "I take it you know who I am."

"Oh yes. When Miss Young informed me you were coming, I prayed I'd have the honor of meeting you in person." The redhead put her hands to her heart and grinned. "I feel so blessed right now."

Brad only smiled, puzzled that he felt such an intense attraction toward her. Sure, the girl had red hair like Amy, but damn, there was something about the woman... Females didn't normally have this effect on him.

"Would you prefer to wait for Carl in the private room?"

"Yes, please," he said with a chuckle, daring to gaze into those baby blues again. There was so much depth to her soul—and a hint of sadness that beckoned to him.

In response to the unusual intensity of his stare, the redhead blushed a deeper shade of pink, which only added to her charm.

The young woman led him to the private room that looked more like a scene from a tropical movie with its lava rocks, miniature waterfall, and lush plants. She pointed to the long leather table in the center. "If you would undress completely and lie face down, Carl should be here shortly."

Being asked to undress by her naturally sultry voice had an unwanted effect. Brad nodded, grateful she would be leaving the room before his attraction to her was more noticeable.

She handed him a small silk cover, and it wasn't until then that Brad noticed how unusually slender her wrist was. Although her frame was hidden under her loose smock, it was obvious the girl was underweight. He felt a sense of protectiveness rise up in him.

"Please use this as a cover-up while you wait, Master Anderson."

He was surprised to hear the word *Master* come from her lips but assumed it had been a slip on her part as he studied her face. He could detect no flirtatious intent as he watched her go to leave the room. "Wait. I don't think I caught your name."

"My name is Shey Allen." She surprised him by quickly apologizing. "My da is Irish and always wanted a boy, so I was blessed with a man's name."

"Shey," he repeated, liking the sound of it. "It fits you well, Miss Allen. You should never apologize for such a charming name."

Her lashes fluttered at the unexpected compliment. "You're very kind. I'll keep that in mind. Thank you."

Turning down the light, Shey left him staring at the door as she quietly left.

Brad wondered if the woman had any idea how striking she was. He shook his head to clear it as he undressed. Once naked, he picked up the small cover-up and laughed, tossing it to the side.

He was not a man who was ashamed of his body. Settling down on the table, he laid his head onto the padded cutout and closed his eyes.

The sound of the trickling water filled the small room, soothing the sexual tension that meeting Shey had caused. Soon he felt himself relaxing and let out a long drawn-out sigh, grateful he'd chosen to splurge by coming to the Nyte Hotel.

Sometimes money *could* buy happiness…

After an extraordinarily long wait, the door finally

opened. Brad didn't bother looking up, choosing instead to remain in his relaxed position. He listened to the man wash his hands, and a few minutes later, hot oil splashed on his skin.

Brad let out a low groan as he worked the oil in. "That feels great, Carl."

The man definitely had magical fingers, just as Francesca had promised. Powerful and strong, but experienced enough to soon have Brad feeling like a puddle of relaxed goo.

A light tapping on his thigh let him know he needed to turn over. Brad did so reluctantly, feeling so comfortable that he didn't have the will to move. Turning onto his back, he suddenly found himself staring straight into those familiar blue eyes.

"What the..." he grumbled, bolting up as he covered his groin with his hands before she could sneak a glance.

"I'm so sorry, Master Anderson! Carl had a family emergency and was forced to leave unexpectedly. Knowing how long you've been waiting, I hated the thought of canceling your appointment."

"Miss Allen, while I appreciate your willingness to take care of my needs, I specifically asked for a male, and you are definitely *not* a man."

"I'm a professional, Mr. Anderson. I *never* overstep the bounds as a masseuse, if that is your concern."

"It is not *you* I'm concerned about," he growled, reaching over and grabbing the small cover-up to place over his hardening shaft. The thin material only helped to emphasize the rigidness of it.

Brad lay back down, seeing the humor in the situation. He stared up at the ceiling with a smirk on his face. Sometimes life was a series of comical curveballs…

"I deeply apologize, Mr. Anderson," she sputtered. "Please know I only desired to honor your appointment. I'll leave, if you prefer."

He could hear guilt tainting her voice, knowing she had displeased him.

"You may stay," he stated, steeling himself for the sexual tension that was already building.

She's a professional, he reminded himself.

Brad closed his eyes again and soon felt the warm oil drip onto his pecs. Her delicate but exceedingly strong fingers had him quietly groaning as she kneaded out the knots of his tension-ridden body.

Taking over The Submissive Training Center as the new headmaster was adding a whole new level of anxiety on top of the already stressful relocation. He was eternally grateful Marquis Gray, with all his years of experience as a trainer at the school, still remained part of the staff—he trusted that it would make the transition smoother for everyone.

Brad became distracted from his wandering thoughts when Shey began massaging the palm of his hand. It was strangely intimate and sensual even though it wasn't intended to be, causing feelings he did not care to deal with. He gently pulled his hand away, muttering, "I could do without that, Miss Allen."

Shey stammered an apology and started on his feet next. Her fingers began their magic as she caressed the balls of his feet, but it caused the same reaction, and he sat up abruptly. "I think we're done here."

She looked crushed. "I'm sorry I failed in my job to-night."

Moving stiffly because of his hard cock, Brad turned his back to her but said in a reassuring tone, "It is not a case of failing, Miss Allen. The fact is, you're a little too skilled with those hands of yours."

He heard her washing up before she headed toward the door. "I'll leave you to dress."

Brad quickly slipped on his sweats, overcome with an irresistible urge to stop her from leaving the room. "Why don't we have dinner tonight? When does your shift end?"

She looked at him in surprise. "Actually, I was off two hours ago. I only stayed to take care of you."

Her answer moved him. As he placed his black Stetson on his head, he winked at her. "All the more reason I owe you a meal and conversation, darlin'."

Shey's pink lips curled into a joyous smile, her blue eyes sparkling. "No need, Master Anderson. It was my pleasure to serve you."

Lord help me, he groaned to himself, imagining her kneeling on the floor after saying that exact phrase, come dripping from her mouth.

Brad knew that dinner with her was a terrible idea. Spending additional time with the girl would only be asking for trouble, but—just like with Amy—he felt defenseless against the powerful attraction he had toward Shey.

One thing was different, however. He'd learned his lesson with Amy. His mistake had been in trying to dominate the redhead into loving him, and he'd come excruciatingly close… God, his heart still ached remembering that day. That horrible moment when Amy had walked away from him and into the arms of Troy Dawson.

Not wanting to repeat the past, Brad determined to keep tonight casual. He actually liked the idea of getting to know Shey on a more personal level, but resolved to make a hasty retreat as soon as dinner was over.

All he wanted was a good night's sleep, and there was a soft bed beckoning to him upstairs. Brad glanced down at his aching cock, which urged him to do otherwise.

Too bad.

His freaking dick could wait for a quick hand job in the shower. There was *no* need to complicate things for either of them.

"Do you mind if I go home to change, Mr. Anderson? I could be back here in less than an hour."

"You look good as you are, Miss Allen, but if it would make you feel better, I have no objections to meeting in an hour."

"Great!" Shey started to walk away, but turned and asked hesitantly, "Do you mind if I dress up? I rarely have the chance."

He furrowed his brow. "I find that hard to believe but, by all means, feel free to dress to the nines."

She nodded and walked away with a pleased smile. He couldn't stop his eyes from drifting to her swaying ass as she left.

Oh, holy hell…

Brad had not planned on going out, and only had

jeans and a T-shirt packed. Making his way to the closest clothing shop in the hotel, he picked out a simple, overpriced suit, shirt, and tie. He then went up to his room, tossed his cowboy hat on a chair, and collapsed onto the bed, wanting to close his eyes for a half-hour.

Cayenne would have none of it and jumped onto his chest, happy that he was back. She rubbed her cheek against his rough chin, purring softly.

He petted her small furry feline frame. "Missed me, huh?"

In answer, she touched her cold nose against his.

Brad chuckled. "Not sure what I would do without your impish ways, Cayenne. I'm grateful young Brie brought us together. Everyone should have a companion like you in their life."

The kitten purred even louder, closing her eyes in ecstasy when he rubbed his finger under her chin.

He lay there enjoying the soothing sound of the unique waterfall wall and his cat's audible joy. Finally, after glancing at the clock, he groaned and reluctantly picked her up, placing her on the feather pillow.

"I shouldn't be long," he assured the kitten as he stripped out of his sweats and donned the gray suit. He pulled down the cuffs of the starched white shirt after he put on the jacket and stood in front of the mirror. "What do you think, girl?"

The tabby jumped off the bed to rub against his pant leg, leaving strands of fur behind. Brad stooped down and did his best to brush them off. "Marking your territory, I see."

He stood back up and stared at his reflection. Saying

good-bye to Colorado hadn't been easy, and it was reflected in his face. Straightening his tie, Brad decided tonight was exactly what he needed.

"Life shouldn't be full of regret…"

A Little Bet

S hey was standing at the bar with her back to him. Her long black dress caressed her curves beautifully, but it was the cutouts at the shoulders showing off her freckled skin that about did him in.

Damn! That girl wasn't making this easy.

Brad walked up without Shey noticing and looked over the drink menu before telling the bartender, "I'll take a Royal Fuck, and why not make one for the pretty lady?"

Shey turned to him, ready to protest, and then giggled when she saw he was the one who'd ordered it. "No need to buy me a drink, Mr. Anderson."

"Nonsense, Miss Allen. I don't care to fuck alone."

She laughed and cordially accepted the drink he handed her. "Although life has a way of doing a fine job of it on its own, here's to being royally bleeped together, Mr. Anderson."

He was grateful to see she had a sense of humor. "Please call me Brad."

"Oh no. That's much too informal. I couldn't…"

49

"Why?" he asked, suddenly suspicious. "Do you have a boyfriend, Miss Allen?"

"I do," she answered, blushing deeply when she admitted it.

"Ah…" Brad took a sip of his drink, actually grateful that was the case. It made tonight so much easier and less complicated. Until the vixen added…

"It's my cat, Troy."

Brad did a spit take, and grunted as he wiped his mouth. "Did I hear you right? You have a cat named Troy?"

She shrugged. "Yep, been with me for over ten years. My best friend and confidant."

"Who names a cat *Troy*?" he asked in disgust.

Shey lifted her chin. "What's wrong with the name Troy?"

"Everything…" he mumbled to himself.

"Would you have preferred I called him Garfield?"

"Is he a fat orange tabby?"

"Orange, yes. Fat, no. However, he does have a thing for lasagna," she answered with a grin.

"Interesting, Miss Allen. I happen to have an orange tabby myself."

Her eyes lit up. "You do?"

"Yes, but she's just a little thing."

"And her name?"

"Cayenne."

Shey cooed out loud. "Oh, that's an adorable name."

"She's quite the character, too."

"Wouldn't it be fun to see the two of them together?"

Brad frowned. "Sorry, Cayenne has zero tolerance for cats named Troy."

"Hey! What's your issue with my cat's name?" Shey demanded, sounding a tad ticked off.

Brad only laughed, lifting his glass and clinking it against hers. "No sense going into *that* tonight. I'd like to enjoy our evening together."

"Fair enough." Shey took a small sip of her drink, leaving red lipstick on the rim of the glass. Brad found the feminine imprint on the clear glass appealing. Raising an eyebrow, he asked, "Is that Royal Fuck living up to your expectations?"

Shey only nodded, her cheeks turning an attractive shade of red.

Brad downed his drink quickly and stood up, holding out his arm to her. "Shall we head out then, darlin'?"

She looked him up and down, checking out his outfit before taking his arm. "The suit suits you, Mr. Anderson."

He chuckled. "You're looking mighty dapper yourself, Miss Allen. However, I insist you call me Brad the rest of the evening." He forced himself to ignore the increase in blood pressure when she wrapped her arm around his.

When they were seated at the table, he casually asked, "So, what looks good on the menu?"

She perused it and purred. "Everything."

Brad let out a sigh of relief. "Good, I was afraid you might be one of those women who only nibble on rabbit food."

She put down her menu and laughed. "Not at all. I

love good food, I just don't have the opportunity to go out much."

Rather than asking why, and sticking his nose where it didn't belong, Brad stated, "Order anything on the menu. I dare you to splurge."

He watched Shey intently as they dined together, noting her subtle body language—the dilated pupils, the licking of her lips, the casual caress of her neck, and the way she leaned in every time he spoke. Every action betrayed her attraction to him, even though she refrained from blatantly flirting.

It was her unconscious flirtation that made her that much more captivating. With those enchanting blue eyes, and that light sprinkling of freckles across her nose, he was completely taken by her—and the girl didn't even know it.

After he'd paid the check, Brad found he wasn't ready to part ways just yet. "Are you a betting woman, Miss Allen?"

She grinned but shook her head. "No, I'm not much of a gambler but I like to play cards."

"Want to have a little fun?"

She looked into his eyes, as if she were trying to read his intentions, before answering, "Sure."

"Ever play stud poker? I personally believe you don't really know a person until you play poker against him."

Her smile broadened. "That would be lovely. You see, my daddy taught me how to play when I was a little kid."

Brad rubbed his hands together. "Then this should be fun…"

He pressed his hand against the small of her back as he guided her into the casino. He enjoyed the attention as every head turned to take in the gorgeous redhead by his side. When they approached an open table, Shey suddenly stopped and whispered, "Brad, I don't have the money to bet."

"No worries," he assured her. "This is my treat."

She shook her head. "As kind as your offer is, I wouldn't enjoy gambling with your money. It's not the same."

Brad nodded in understanding. "I see your point. Just a moment, I'll be right back." He went to speak to the pit boss. After making the necessary arrangements, he came back to her and explained, "Ms. Browne has agreed to secure us a private table where money won't be used as collateral."

Shey tilted her head. "What do you mean, 'money won't be the collateral'?"

"To make it interesting, I thought we'd bet requests rather than cash, and whoever wins the hand gets their bid fulfilled by the other player."

Shey looked at him suspiciously. "Although I respect you, Brad, I hardly know you. Why would I ever put myself in that position?"

"I've already considered that. For your peace of mind, we'll have a third party at the table. Ms. Browne suggested Wesley Tate. Are you familiar with the man?"

Shey giggled. "Mr. Tate? He's the front desk manager and is a perfect choice for such an event."

"Excellent. I'll order up a couple of drinks while Ms. Browne gets things set up." He slipped a twenty into the nearest slot machine—an animated game called the Red Phoenix, complete with flaming birds and catchy music. "Why don't you try your luck while I get our cocktails? Consider it a gift to me. I want to see the level of natural luck you possess."

Shey shook her head as she sat down at the machine, mumbling, "Based on my luck these days, I'm sure to have it all lost before you return."

Brad patted her on the shoulder. "I'm actually hoping that's the case, Miss Allen. It will make beating you at poker that much easier."

He'd already thought of a few requests for her, and was looking forward to having them fulfilled. While he was paying for the drinks, Ms. Browne walked over and informed him the private room was ready. He thanked her with a generous tip before heading back to the slots.

To his chagrin, Shey's machine was lit up with fiery phoenixes filling the screen. She jumped up in excitement when she saw him, and pointed at it. "I'm the jackpot winner! Can you believe it? That's two hundred and forty-two green bills, my friend."

Brad took her hand and kissed it formally. "Congrats, Miss Allen. Why don't we cash in your prize before we begin our private game?"

Shey quickly picked up her purse and followed him. "Of course the money is yours—it was your twenty after all."

"Oh, no, the jackpot is yours to keep."

"Please—I can't accept your winnings."

"You can, and you will," he stated kindly. "Seeing the excitement on your face when I walked up was worth the price of admission."

"Does that mean we'll be playing for real money at the table then?" she asked as the cash was counted out and handed to her.

"Absolutely not."

Shey stuffed the bills in her small purse and looked up at him with a gleam in her eye. "I'm glad to hear it. My luck seems to have changed, and there are a few things I'm hoping to win from you tonight."

His laughter filled the air as he escorted her to the private room. "Oh no, darlin'. I'll be the one beating your cute little panties off this evening."

A stylish young man wearing a black suit, red tie, and bright red Superman socks greeted them at the private table.

"It's a pleasure to meet you, Mr. Anderson. I see you've already met the spa siren."

"You mean Miss Allen?"

"Yes, sir. She has the most talented fingers in the business."

Brad gave Shey a sideways glance but refrained from commenting. "I assume Ms. Browne explained the game I've requested tonight?"

Wesley put his hands behind his back and clicked his heels. "She did, and I plan to beat your pants off, Mr. Anderson—literally."

Brad raised his eyebrows. "Really? Only if you have the luck of the Irish, Mr. Tate. You see, I have quite the reputation as a player back in Denver."

Wesley quipped, "I bet you do, *Master* Anderson."

Chuckling as he pulled out the chair for Shey, Brad

held out his other hand to greet the man who would be their dealer for the evening. "Thank you for taking on this unusual game of poker. I assure you it won't get too shocking."

The man smiled politely. "Trust me, Mr. Anderson, at the Nyte we've seen it all."

"And some of us have done it all..." Wesley murmured wickedly.

The dealer asked, "So, Mr. Anderson, what type of poker game are we playing tonight?"

"Stud poker," Brad stated as he took off his jacket and slowly rolled up his sleeves before taking a seat.

"Stud poker, is it?" Wesley looked him over with approval as he took a seat on the other side of Shey. "But of course. What else would a man of your considerable looks play?"

He then turned to Shey and asked, "I trust I'm allowed to bet in this game?"

Shey shrugged her shoulders, deferring to Brad.

It was with amusement that Brad delivered the bad news. "You're simply here to provide a third hand and to act as referee if either of us objects to a bet that's been placed."

"Damn..." Wesley pouted. "I was hoping to have a few wishes of my own fulfilled tonight."

Brad placed his hand over his heart. "Although I don't swing on that branch, I'm truly honored, Mr. Tate."

Wesley grinned charmingly. "You may call me Wes." He turned to Shey and shook his index finger at her. "As I am your superior, you must continue to address me as

Mr. Tate—even if you *are* off the clock."

She bowed her head slightly. "I would never consider calling you anything else, Mr. Tate."

Brad admired her grace—a true lady. *And an easy mark,* he thought with a smirk.

The dealer handed Shey a stack of notecards and two pens while Brad explained to her, "You and I will write down our requests and fold them into fourths. If you think you have a winning hand, you put the request in the middle. After the dealer reveals the other three cards, you have a choice to leave your bet or fold. Whoever has the winning hand wins their bet, unless Wesley's hand beats ours. In that case, you and I will each be required to remove an article of clothing."

Shey protested, "A game of strip poker when you're wearing more clothes than I am?"

"I'm allowing your jewelry to count, Miss Allen."

Shey settled back into her seat, a grin spreading across her face. "Well, fine then. Let the games begin…"

The dealer handed out two cards to each player. Brad watched Shey closely as she took a peek at her hand. He didn't miss the twinkle in her eye as she set them back down. "What are the rules about our bets?"

"Keep them simple and something that can be done tonight."

"Okay. But for the record, intercourse is *not* on the table."

"As you wish…" Brad replied with a mischievous grin.

She looked at him momentarily before scribbling down her request, folding it, and gleefully placing it in the middle of the table.

Brad slowly turned up the edges of his cards, keeping a straight face.

Two deuces.

A pair of any sort wasn't bad, considering only three of them were playing. He wrote down his bet and casually tossed it in the center.

There was no need to bet as each card was revealed, like in a normal hand of poker, so the dealer spread out all three at once after both bets had been placed.

Shey bit her bottom lip as she looked at the cards on the table and then announced confidently, "I'm still in!"

Brad looked the three cards over. They were all the same suit, but there was nothing there to help his hand. Curious to see what Shey was holding, he stated, "I call."

Shey blushed as she flipped over her cards to reveal she had absolutely nothing.

"You little minx," he said in admiration, as he turned over his winning deuces.

All her telltale signs had simply been an act. *Clever girl...*

Brad was about to hand her his request when Wesley stopped him. "Not so fast, Mr. Anderson." With a dramatic flair, he revealed his hand, which only consisted of a four and seven of hearts. That, however, gave him the winning flush.

Wesley raised his eyebrow suggestively. "And you both know what that means..."

Shey immediately removed her earrings and placed them on the table, giggling to herself.

Brad loosened his tie and slid it off, placing it next to

her jewelry. He liked the fact she'd tried to bluff right out of the gate. Now that he knew she was a bluffer, he was certain to win the next hand.

What he hadn't counted on was Wesley's impressive winning streak. The next three hands left Brad shirtless and barefoot, while Shey was free of all jewelry and her heels.

"Either you or I need to win the next hand, Miss Allen."

"You aren't kidding," she laughed nervously, staring hard at the cards that had just been dealt.

When Brad lifted his cards and saw a pair of kings, he knew victory was his. He placed his request on the table and tilted his head. "Are you feeling lucky, Miss Allen?"

Shey glanced at her cards again and nodded. "I am."

The dealer laid out the remaining cards and looked to Brad first. He stared at the six of hearts, the jack of diamonds, and the ten of spades on the table. Nothing posed a threat to his hand. "I'm in," he declared.

Shey stared at the three cards, nervously biting her lip again. She stared at Brad for several seconds, studying his face before proclaiming, "I call."

Brad flipped his cards over.

Wesley threw his hand to the center in disgust, while Shey sat back silently watching them both.

Brad grinned as he handed her his request. "Don't feel bad, darlin'. Someone had to lose."

"Agreed, so I hope you aren't too hard on yourself." She turned her cards over with a triumphant grin. "I believe three of a kind beats a pair."

He stared down at her cards in disbelief. Had she really just played him—again?

Damn…

Brad graciously took her request and unfolded it, frowning when he read what was written.

> Tell me who Troy is and why the name still
> upsets you.

"This is supposed to be a fun evening of gambling, Miss Allen, not a therapy session."

Shey shrugged. "I find it entertaining to learn little-known facts about the men I date."

Brad sighed as he put her bet back on the table. "Because I am a man of my word, I will accept this request, but I'm not happy about it." To the dealer he barked, "Keep dealing."

"But what about my request?" Shey protested.

"It'll be honored after the game."

"Great. That gives me another idea…" she told him, writing down her next one.

Brad was impressed, but exasperated, that she'd manipulated him twice. He snuck a peek at his hand and smiled at her. "The gloves are officially off, missy."

Her delighted giggles filled the room.

It was with immense satisfaction he handed her his first request the very next hand. Brad watched her eyes grow wide when she read it out loud. "A kiss?"

"Just a simple kiss."

"Now?"

He leaned in close, his lips dangerously close to hers.

She closed her eyes in anticipation, until he whispered, "No, Miss Allen, after the game is over."

She opened her eyes and pouted. "You are a wicked man, Brad Anderson."

Several consecutive wins had him on even ground again, and it was with great joy that he watched Shey's face when Wesley won the next hand.

"I don't know what to do," she whimpered, looking bereft as she contemplated which piece of clothing to take off.

"Your panties would work in a pinch," Brad suggested with a naughty grin. "Allows you to keep your dignity while still honoring the bet."

She nodded, accepting his recommendation. Shey turned away as she carefully removed her underwear without exposing herself. She placed the sexy thong on top of her pile and looked at him expectantly.

Knowing that Shey was bare under that dress was exceedingly hot. He undid his belt and slipped it through the belt loops, taking his time as he rolled it up before dropping it on the table.

He smiled in satisfaction at the sexy clank the buckle made as it landed. "One more hand, Miss Allen?"

Shey's breath increased as she weighed the risks. "Yes, one more."

After looking at their final cards, each of them wrote down a last request. Shey sighed nervously as she placed hers in the middle. Brad noticed that her eyes didn't leave it, even when the dealer laid out the other three cards. Whatever she'd requested had her anxious, and *that* was arousing to him.

Brad stared at the three cards, shocked to see he had a royal flush. He should have been thrilled, but he was far more interested in Shey's request than in winning the hand. "I call."

Shey laid down a pair of threes and looked at him hopefully.

"Damn...you got me beat." Brad tossed his cards to the dealer in mock disgust without revealing them to her.

Shey's hand visibly shook as she handed him her final bet. "Don't read it just yet," she begged.

Brad was willing, but added a stipulation as he held the unopened request up. "Fine. I'll refrain from reading this only if you agree to walk out just as you are."

Her eyes darted to Wesley, who nodded. She looked down at her bare feet, the only part of her body that was exposed, and shrugged. "Deal."

Brad tucked her last bet in his pocket while Wesley quickly gathered up their clothing. Mr. Tate stood before Brad, his eyes transfixed on Brad's bare chest. "I'd be honored to escort you to your room, Mr. Anderson."

"Much appreciated."

Brad turned to the dealer and handed him a tip. "Thank you for your help tonight."

"My pleasure, sir."

Brad walked out of the room proudly, baring his muscular chest to the world with a beautiful, elegantly dressed—and deliciously barefoot—redhead wrapped on his arm.

Play in the casino stopped for a moment as the two walked through the main floor in their various states of undress. He took pride in the fact that the men were openly gawking at Shey, their facial expressions communicating their admiration of her striking looks.

Wesley guided them to the private staff elevator. It wasn't until the doors finally closed that Shey giggled in relief. "God only knows what they're thinking about us."

"They're thinking I'm one hell of a lucky guy," Brad stated.

Shey snorted daintily. "No, the women were definitely thinking, 'Who the hell is that hunk of a man and how do I tap me some of that?'"

Brad's booming laughter filled the elevator. "Trust me, Shey, all eyes were on you."

Wesley's eyes returned to Brad's chest for a moment before he glanced away.

"Exactly," Shey stated in triumph. "Even Mr. Tate agrees."

Brad turned to Shey and casually rubbed his hand over his pecs, watching with amusement as her eyes widened while they followed the movement, almost as if she were in a trance. When the doors opened, she started, the spell suddenly broken.

Wesley held the elevator as the two exited and followed them, but Shey stopped abruptly.

"Brad, I'm not sure…"

She looked like she was about to bolt, so he placed his hand on her arm to reassure her. "Not sure of what, Miss Allen?"

"If I'm ready for this."

"Every request will be honored to your complete satisfaction. I am a gentleman, after all."

She let out a nervous sigh. "*Every* one?"

That final, unknown bet of Shey's burned like fire in his pocket and had him totally distracted. Brad fiddled with it, wondering what the hell she'd asked of him that had her so on edge.

He leaned forward and whispered so only she could hear. "First, I'd like to show you my little orange pussy, Miss Allen."

Shey looked stunned. "Are you saying what I think you're saying?"

Brad put his finger to his lips. "Shh…it's our little secret."

She tsked, but there was a mischievous glint in her eyes as she glanced in Wesley's direction. "Well, Mr. Anderson, I would definitely like to see that."

"Then you shall…"

Wesley tried to hide his smile, chuckling to himself as he handed Mr. Anderson their clothes. "A night at the Nyte is *never* boring."

"Thank you for your assistance tonight, Mr. Tate."

Brad tried to hand the man a tip, but Wesley refused it. "No, Mr. Anderson. I was happy to act as the third hand to your unique poker game."

He abruptly turned and clicked his heels, drawing attention to his red Superman socks as he entered the elevator. "Please enjoy the rest of your evening." He added a respectful nod to Shey as the doors closed.

Brad looked down at her and smiled. "Are you ready to have all your wishes fulfilled, Miss Allen?"

Honoring a Wish

S hey bit her lip as the double doors to his suite slowly opened, and she hesitantly stepped inside. She glanced around the spacious room with a look of wonder on her face.

"Haven't you ever seen this room before?" Brad asked, surprised by her response.

Shey shook her head. "Oh no, the fantasy suites are off-limits to the staff unless we reserve them for ourselves." She gravitated to the lighted waterfall wall, running her hands over the glass. "It's spectacular…"

"A favorite feature of mine."

She peeked into the dining room on the other side of the doorway and said with awe, "Can you imagine eating in here? A waterfall on one side and all of Vegas on the other."

He came up behind her, tempted to wrap his arms around her waist. Although she was in his hotel room, tonight was not destined to end in a sexual encounter. There was no reason to seduce Shey, but damn, how he wanted to try.

She turned to face him, a suspicious look on her face. "I'm not seeing any sign of Cayenne. Were you just using her as an excuse to get me into your room?"

Brad glanced around. "Apparently she's afraid of you, Miss Allen."

"No, cats love me!" she protested, searching through the entire suite before heading toward the large bed. She got on all fours to look under it, that sweet ass of hers tempting him to act. To his credit, Brad resisted the call and remained rooted where he stood.

"There you are," Shey cooed sweetly.

Cayenne came shooting out from under the bed, scampering straight to Brad and clawing her way up the pant leg of his new suit.

Shey squeaked in delight. "Oh my goodness, she's adorable!"

Once Cayenne reached his shoulder, she turned around to face Shey directly, studying her with wide eyes. He scooped the kitten off his shoulder and cradled her to his chest. "Let me formally introduce you two. This is my companion, Cayenne. Cayenne, this is the beautiful and talented Miss Allen."

Shey walked over and reached her hand out to the tabby, letting the kitten sniff her before petting her head. She murmured, "You can call me Shey."

"The kitten or me?" Brad asked.

Shey glanced up and grinned. "Both."

"So be it…Miss Shey Allen."

She blushed when she met his gaze.

Like it or not, he was already falling for the girl, and it appeared little Cayenne was, too. The kitten crawled out of his arms and into hers, settling against her shoulder.

"Seems Cayenne has taken a liking to you."

"I told you cats love me," she purred as she petted the tiny kitten.

Brad's curiosity finally won out, so he dug into his pocket and pulled out her final request along with the others.

"We should read them out loud," Shey suggested, selecting Brad's requests from his palm while being careful not to disturb Cayenne. "A simple kiss…" She glanced at Brad with a shy smile before reading the next. "What is your favorite drink?" She raised an eyebrow at him. "Why do you want to know? Do you intend on getting me drunk?"

"Not at all, Shey," he said, chuckling. "I naturally assumed we would remain down in the casino and thought to myself, 'What better way to loosen up the conversation than by sharing a favorite cocktail together?'"

"Fair enough…" she conceded. Shey unfolded his last one, biting her lip as she glanced over it.

"Read it out loud," he commanded.

She looked at him and said in a breathless whisper, "Place your hand on the area you want me to touch you."

Brad stared at her, pleased to see she was completely unraveled by his final request. He knew that giving Shey a choice would not only give her a feeling of control, but would also allow him to gauge her level of interest.

It was a win for them both.

To ease her mind, however, he explained, "Since I have had the pleasure of your magic fingers, I decided turnabout is fair play."

"Ah," she replied distractedly, playing with a strand of her hair.

A good sign…

Impatient to discover what her last request was, Brad quickly read through the others. "So you asked me to tell you who Troy is and why I dislike the name." He snorted in disgust, grumbling, "I'm not so keen on that particular request."

Shey smiled sweetly, the picture of mischievous innocence. "Lucky for you, we'll be drinking our favorite cocktails."

He shook his head in amusement as he read the next one. "I would like to see a picture of Cayenne."

Brad gestured to the kitten, who was now purring contentedly on her shoulder. "Why show you a picture when I could let you see the real thing?"

Shey scratched the top of Cayenne's head, laughing softly. "I can't believe you smuggled a kitten into the hotel. Miss Young would completely flip if she knew."

Brad only smiled, keeping that little secret to himself as he unfolded her final bet. He could feel the weight of Shey's eyes on him as he read it.

Do a scene with me – your choice.

He looked up from the note, saying nothing.

The redhead blushed a deeper shade of crimson with each passing second, finally lowering her gaze to the floor in embarrassment.

"Yes, Shey. I will scene with you not only to honor our bet, but because it pleases me." When she looked up, Brad took his hat off and leaned in for a kiss, pressing his lips against hers.

Shey's whole body seemed to meld into his, a soft moan escaping from her lips. He pulled away, unnerved by the power of that kiss.

She stared up at him with a stunned look in those luminous blue eyes. "That was…"

"What?" Brad reached out and grazed her bottom lip. "Too much?"

"No." Shey smiled. "It was perfect."

The intensity of his attraction was disquieting. He was haunted by the idea that if he dared to have another taste, he would hunger for this woman the rest of his life.

Feeling reckless, however, he asked, "Why don't you tell me your favorite drink."

"I'm a long island girl."

"Ah…a deceptively easy drink to swallow, but with quite the kick—much like you."

She grinned, apparently liking his comparison. "What is your drink of choice?"

"Me? I prefer whiskey, neat."

"Oh, you like it simple, then."

Brad shrugged. "What can I say? I know what I like, and I don't want it messed with."

"Drinking whiskey does make you seem more rugged."

He smirked. "I believe what a person drinks gives insight into their personality."

"Are you always analyzing people, Brad?"

"Only people I'm interested in."

The smile she bestowed on him was beguiling. Too beguiling...

Brad walked over to the phone to place their drink order, instructing the staff, "Come up with a second round exactly thirty minutes from now."

"Two rounds?" Shey questioned when he got off the phone.

"First one to loosen me up to talk, and the second to enjoy."

Not more than five minutes later, there was a brisk knock at the door. Cayenne jumped from Shey's arms and scampered under the bed.

"God, I love good service," Brad praised as he walked over to answer the door.

"Only the best at the Nyte," Shey stated proudly.

A young woman in an attractive waitress uniform, complete with short skirt and high heels, stood waiting at the door. "Where would you like it, Mr. Anderson?"

"Over there," he said, pointing to the dining table beyond the waterfall. She walked into the room with grace, setting their drinks on the table before returning to him. He handed her a generous tip, stating, "I admire a girl who doesn't spill a drop."

Giving him a small curtsy, she thanked him before leaving.

Brad escorted Shey into the dining room and pulled out a seat for her.

"Why, thank you, Mr. Anderson," she said formally, her tone matching the elegant setting.

"My pleasure, Miss Allen." He pushed her chair in before handing her the Long Island and picking up his glass of whiskey, raising it to her. "Here's to honoring a bet."

Shey smiled as she placed those sexy lips against the rim of the glass.

Brad couldn't help envisioning those fine lips wrapped around his manhood, so he threw back his glass and downed the drink, shaking his head afterward to rid himself of the unwanted thought.

"Too strong?" she teased.

Brad pulled out the chair beside her and turned it around, quickly sitting down to hide his "growing" interest in her.

"You asked about my aversion to the name Troy. I personally can't stand sob stories on a first date, so I'll keep it short." He groaned before continuing, wishing she hadn't asked this of him. Talking about Amy when the pain was still fresh—but a bet was a bet.

"I met Amy Gardner years ago. At that time I was determined to make a name for myself in Denver—both professionally in the business sector, and personally as a Dom." He added with a smirk, "I was a far more serious man back then."

"Well, you certainly did make a name for yourself," Shey complimented, raising her glass to him as she took another drink.

He looked at his empty glass longingly, wishing he'd ordered a double. "Up until Amy, I hadn't known what it was like to actually love someone. Lust, yes—in spades—but never love. Although she wasn't interested in exploring the lifestyle, I was convinced she was meant to be *my* submissive."

He closed his eyes, shaking his head. Damn, it still hurt...

Brad forced his eyes open and gazed into Shey's blue oceans. "To make a long story short, I wasn't aware that she'd had her heart broken and still secretly carried a torch for the guy. Just when I thought she was mine, he returned, and poof—I lost her."

"Am I wrong to assume the guy's name was Troy?"

He growled upon hearing that name. "And to add salt to the wound, a year later I found out that Amy had been in a serious accident and he was nowhere to be found. I went to the hospital, determined not to lose her again, but I made the mistake of compromising myself in trying to claim her. In the end, I made a fool of myself for nothing, and was burned a second time."

"So I take it Troy returned?" Shey prompted gently when he failed to explain further.

"Yes," he huffed. "In fact, she was wearing my engagement ring when he showed up."

Shey surprised Brad by wrapping her arms around him, her voice breaking with emotion when she said, "I'm so sorry, Brad."

Her expression of sympathy threw him off, and Brad felt tears suddenly well up in his eyes. He resisted them, having already said good-bye to his past. Still, her heartfelt response moved him deeply. When he looked into Shey's tearful eyes and saw the pain reflected in them, he finally understood why.

"You've been hurt in the same way."

Shey nodded, a sob escaping her lips. "Although I never wore his ring, Sam promised to marry me. Instead, he married *her*, and to make matters worse, the girl's already pregnant with their first child. That was supposed to be *my* little girl."

"What was her name—the one who stole him away?"

"Laura…" Shey answered in the barest of whispers.

He took her hand and kissed it. "I solemnly promise never to name my cat Laura."

Shey burst into giggles as she wiped away her tears. "And I officially give you permission to call my cat T."

"T it is, then."

Brad gathered Shey into his arms, both silent as they basked in the easy camaraderie between them.

Shey jumped when there was a knock on the door.

Looking at his watch, Brad complimented, "Exactly thirty minutes to the dot. You can't beat the staff here." This time Brad took the tray from the waitress, thanking her as he handed over another tip. "Exacting service should always be rewarded."

"Much appreciated, Mr. Anderson," she replied with a cute curtsy, closing the doors as he made his way back to Shey.

Brad handed her the second glass. "Don't feel you have to drink this. I tend to err on the side of overabundance rather than risk being caught short. It's something my mother taught me growing up. During our leaner years, she still managed to have a full table, even if it consisted mainly of homemade rolls and mashed potatoes."

"A woman after my own heart..." she replied, taking a sip of the fresh drink.

Brad's tone became serious when he told her, "Before I fulfill your final request, I want you to honor mine."

She put her drink down slowly. Brad noticed the slight tremble of her hand as she placed it on the table.

"Do you remember what it was, Shey?"

"I do."

Brad moved closer to her, purposely invading her space. "Take my hand."

She looked up at him shyly. Being in control was not something she seemed accustomed to. Would she be true to her desire, or would she choose to be modest with him?

Shey finally took his hand and placed it against her throat. "I'd like you to kiss me."

Brad's shaft stirred at the suggestion. Caressing her throat gently, as if it were a prized piece of art, he found the perfect spot. Goosebumps rose on her skin when he applied pressure, letting him know the intimate touch was having the desired effect.

"You want me to kiss you?" he growled huskily, drawing closer to her lips.

"Yes..."

Her whole body relaxed, an instinctual reaction to the dominant hold. He leaned down to kiss her, claiming her lips as he pressed his hand against her throat firmly. She moaned when his tongue entered her mouth.

Brad suspected if he were to place his hand between her legs he would find her wet with desire. He eventually pulled away and stared at her intently. Shey opened her eyes, an expression of pure lust shining in them.

"I never knew a kiss could be like that," she confessed.

"Why? Those lips would inspire any man."

She grazed her soft lips with her fingers, shaking her head slowly. "No. Trust me, no man has ever been *that* inspired before."

Brad leaned down again, giving the impression he was going to kiss her a second time. Instead, he gave her a quick peck on the nose and chuckled lightly. "You've obviously been hanging with the wrong men, Shey Allen."

She grinned, trying nonchalantly to cross her legs and hide the fact that her pussy was deliciously wet.

With his last request fulfilled, it was time to honor hers. "If I'm to satisfy your final bet, I need to fetch equipment out of my truck."

Brad could see the nerves hit. Shey held her breath for a moment before answering, "Of course."

He gave a quick whistle, and Cayenne peeked out from under the bed. "Enjoy the company of my feline companion while I fetch the required items."

He liked the idea of leaving Shey alone with abundant time to anticipate their scene together. Those prolonged minutes of expectation would enrich her overall experience.

Brad knew many Doms were in such a rush to begin a scene that they failed to utilize the simple tool of time. It was a shame, because it not only added to the scene but immediately established dominance.

After persuading the overly friendly valet to let him get items from the truck himself, Brad made his way to the vehicle and searched through his box of equipment, picking out three different instruments: one for a novice, one if Shey was feeling more adventurous, and the last if she was willing to trust him completely.

Brad chuckled to himself as he stuffed them into a duffle bag. Tonight was proving to be far more interesting than he originally planned—but he was not one to complain. He understood this was a once-in-a-lifetime opportunity to scene with the beautiful redhead.

After tonight, they would go their separate ways...

Submission

B rad stood by the entrance of his suite for a few
moments before opening the doors. He was not
surprised to find Shey standing there waiting for him,
with Cayenne nestled in her arms.

"Kneel," he commanded.

Her eyes widened, but Shey dutifully set the kitten
down and sank to the floor, staring up at him expectantly.

Brad shut the doors behind him, using an authoritative tone when he explained, "Although this won't be a
formal lesson, you will call me Master and I will address
you as slave during tonight's session."

She gave a quick gasp but lowered her head and answered, "Yes, Master."

Hearing those words come from her lips affected
him on a profound level. He realized that he would have
to separate himself emotionally or risk getting caught up
in this scene. Brad placed his hand on her head, her red
locks stirring something primal inside him. "Stand, slave,
and serve your Master."

He felt her quiver under his hand. Shey slowly stood, missing the grace of a trained submissive, but Brad found it charming. He'd always had a special heart for "wild ones".

Although Shey was curious about exploring the lifestyle, she was still an unbroken filly. There was excitement in breaking one in...

"I want you to grab your thong from the table and strip down to only your bra and panties while I dress for play."

"Should I kneel again once I'm done?"

"Excellent question," he complimented, and rewarded her with additional instructions. "You will stand in the entryway to the dining room with your hands and feet touching the gold frame so that you are displayed for my pleasure."

He continued toward the bedroom, grinning to himself. His requested position would give her a similar look to being bound to a St. Andrew's Cross—a sexy presentation for him to enjoy, while also being an exposing stance for her. A good first test...

He returned minutes later, dressed in only loose jeans and his black Stetson.

Shey smiled when she saw him, her gaze locking on his muscular chest before darting to the floor.

Brad strode over to her and lifted her chin. "I like my slaves to look at me at all times—unless I command otherwise."

She raised those baby blues to him, and his heart skipped a beat. There was something sacred and hallowed about scening with a brand-new submissive.

Feigning control he did not feel, Brad backed away to study her, looking Shey over with the critical eye of a Master.

She was gripping the frame of the doorway with both hands, her legs spread apart so that her feet touched it as well. If she had been a properly trained sub, she would have stood on tiptoes to make the pose even more enticing for him.

He was pleased to see that the redhead had chosen to wear a sexy underwear set. The bra showed off Shey's petite but attractive breasts, and the thong was secured with an enticing bow. One pull, and it would reveal the treasure hidden underneath. A silent invitation…

Brad enjoyed analyzing a woman's lingerie, because it revealed her tastes and confidence level. Ill-fitting lingerie hinted at a lack of appreciation for her own body, while an overly ornamental set hinted at a need to impress—and "grandma" underwear let a man know exactly where he stood.

Shey's simple-but-playful choice was a winning combination. Although the bow was tempting, he refrained from baring the beauty it concealed so enticingly.

"Are you familiar with safewords, slave?"

"Yes…Master."

"And they are?"

"*Green* if I enjoy it, *yellow* if it's a little too much, and *red* if I want you to stop."

"Very good. Although I will ask throughout the session, it's your duty to call out if there is a need at any point during our scene. Since we are new to each other, it's essential that I can trust you to do that."

Shey nodded, gazing deep into his eyes for added emphasis. "I promise to call out my safeword if needed."

"I will hold you to that, young slave. Knowing this is your first time, I've brought a variety of instruments. Since you gave me the choice, I picked three."

"Three?" she questioned anxiously, fear beginning to surface.

Brad chuckled, understanding the reason for her nerves, and informed her, "I brought three so that you may choose the one that calls to you."

She visibly relaxed, curiosity replacing her fear.

Brad reached into his bag and held up the blindfold first.

Shey frowned, clearly unimpressed. "That's just for vanilla girls."

He shook his head. "You are wrong, slave. There is a high level of kink to be enjoyed when wearing a blindfold with a stranger."

Her eyes widened as the truth of his words sank in. She stared at the simple cloth with newfound respect.

Brad reached back into his duffle bag and held up a set of nipple clamps attached with a delicate chain. "If you are unfamiliar with the instrument, it can seem intimidating. However, the chain allows for self-pleasure, which is something I enjoy watching."

Shey stared at the jeweled clamps he held in his hand. He noticed her body betray her interest: her nipples hardening into tight buds, beckoning to be caressed and teased.

He laid the clamps beside the blindfold and reached into the bag again. "Your last choice is a tool that's a hard limit for many. Don't feel ashamed if you have no interest in it. This is not something a Dominant would normally use on a new sub. However, my proficiency with this tool allows me to offer the option to you tonight."

Brad slowly pulled out his leather bullwhip and smiled in satisfaction as the pupils of her eyes grew.

He unfurled the whip so she could see the full length of it before telling her, "This is a miniature version, specifically crafted for indoor play. It has the capability to lick your skin or draw blood, depending on the strength of the stroke."

Her eyes remained focused on it, but he was unable to tell whether her interest was out of fascination or fear.

"Would you like to hold it, slave?"

Shey nodded slowly as she held out her hands. She took the leather whip and caressed it with delicate fingers, taking in the supple give of the thong and fall. She charmed him when she brushed her cheek with the end, smiling. "I didn't expect it to have a tickly part."

"That's called the cracker," he explained. "It only tickles if I let it."

Shey let the end fall from her hand and stared at him thoughtfully, saying nothing.

"So, slave, which tool do you choose?"

She seriously contemplated each one before asking humbly, "May I have all three?"

He had to stop his jaw from dropping. It was the last answer he expected to hear.

"Unless, of course, that is not allowed," she amended when he failed to respond.

Brad thought a moment before answering. "I have used all three in scenes before, but *not* with a novice. You may be biting off more than you can chew, young lady."

Shey said earnestly, "I find the mystery that the blindfold will inspire enchanting, and I've always wanted to try nipple clamps. However, this bullwhip thrills me in a way I haven't experienced before." She handed him the whip before putting her hands back on the frame and smiling at him.

Brad tilted his head. The redhead had surprised him with her self-confidence. Normally, he'd never suggest the use of all three instruments with a beginner, but her conviction and reasoning seemed sound.

"Don't forget your safeword, slave."

Shey's face lit up when she realized he was agreeing to her wishes. "I won't...Master."

Brad picked up the blindfold and saw Shey's chest begin to quickly rise and fall as he approached her—the reality of what she was about to experience finally kicking in. He wouldn't hold it against the girl if she called out her safeword. New submissives often fantasized about scenes they were unable to handle in real life.

Placing the silk material over her eyes and securing it tightly, he asked in a low voice, "Can you see, slave?"

She visibly trembled when she answered him. "No."

"No, *Master*."

Shey immediately corrected herself, a blush darkening her cheeks.

Brad lightly touched her bare shoulder, tracing the freckles that had tempted him all night.

She tensed under his caress.

He lowered his head, hesitating a moment before pressing his firm lips against a freckle.

The redhead let out a tiny gasp—the intensity of the contact heightened by the blindfold. He pulled away to observe her again.

There was no denying he was extremely turned on by the sight of this girl blindfolded and nearly naked before him. He looked down at his crotch and shook his head in sympathy at the large bulge straining in his pants. Sadly, his cock would have to remain unutilized to avoid unnecessary entanglements between them.

Brad lightly kissed her skin and was rewarded with a whisper of a moan. Unable to resist, he lifted her chin and kissed Shey on the mouth, parting her lips with his tongue. When she pressed her body against him, he ceased holding himself back and ravaged her mouth, leaving her panting for breath afterward.

She was not the only one affected by the passionate kiss... Although Shey was a novice, her instinctual response to him had Brad's body aching to fuck her— but giving in to that carnal desire would only lead to trouble.

He had to remain vigilant for both their sakes.

Brad commanded her to stay as he retrieved his second glass of whiskey and downed it. *Tread carefully*, he warned himself.

He wanted Shey to leave with a healthy appreciation for the Master/slave dynamic, so he chose to approach their encounter in the same manner he would as headmaster of The Submissive Training Center.

"Slave, I want you to drop on all fours and crawl

over to me. Entice me with your sensual advance."

Shey lowered herself to the floor and turned toward the sound of his voice. She arched her back before starting forward. It was obvious she was unaware that her tongue was sticking out of the side of her mouth as she concentrated on crawling across the floor for him, but Brad found it charming.

There was something beautiful about a woman's first submissive experience. Their lack of confidence, along with their eagerness to please, was an honor to behold. It was the reason he enjoyed seeking and taming the "wild ones".

As Shey drew closer, he complimented, "Very nice, slave."

She stopped when she reached his feet and knelt again, tilting her head upward in expectation.

Brad leaned down and took one of her wrists, guiding her hand to his raging hard-on. "That is my response to your effort."

She bit her lip and smiled, obviously pleased with herself. There was no doubt the redhead was every bit as turned on as he was.

"Stand up before me, and take off your bra."

Shey stood and fumbled at the clasp, betraying her building nerves.

"Do you need help with such a simple command, slave?" he asked teasingly.

"No, Master," she assured him, continuing to struggle with it.

He watched as her breasts swelled over the top of her bra as she reached back farther, straining to release them without assistance. Just when he was about to do it for her, Shey undid the clasp, and the satin material fell away, exposing her rosy pink nipples. She let the bra fall to the floor but self-consciously crossed her arms over her chest.

"No, slave, your Master wants to enjoy your breasts."

She let her arms fall to her sides but stood trembling as he took in her naked chest. Her unconscious modesty was enchanting, serving to highlight her inexperience.

Shey's creamy white skin accentuated the rosiness of her areolas. "You are truly beautiful."

She bowed her head, trying to hide her smile.

When Brad placed his large hand on one breast, he felt Shey's entire body stiffen and heard her sharp intake of breath. A stranger touching a private part of her femininity was enough to excite any woman.

He caressed her hardening nipple with his thumb. "Your body reveals your need for the clamps, slave."

Shey nodded as she licked her lips nervously.

The tweezer clamps made a delicate clinking sound when he picked up the chain. He noticed the goose-bumps rise on the girl's skin as she anxiously awaited the clamps' unique touch.

Pinching her areola lightly so that her nipple pro-truded, Brad applied the first clamp, adjusting it until she felt the pressure. "Is it comfortable?"

Shey smiled and nodded.

Brad adjusted it even tighter until she gasped but, to her credit, she did not protest. "Your body needs to adjust to it," he assured her, kissing her gently on the lips.

He watched as her nipple turned a dark shade of red under the instrument's constriction. With a mischievous grin, he began playing with her other breast, noting her rapidly beating heart under his hand.

The thrill of willing submission was one of the most erotic aspects of being a Dom.

Shey whimpered when he lightly pinched the sensitive skin before applying the other clamp.

"Color, slave?" he asked gruffly.

"Green."

"Excellent." Although she was frightened, the excitement of this new sensation was driving her to explore further. With a gentle touch, he adjusted the second clamp to provide equal pressure with the first.

She tilted her head back, forcing herself to accept the intensity of the instrument.

"That's it," he praised. "Give in to the feeling the clamps evoke."

When he brushed his fingers lightly against her nipples, she cried out.

"Color?" he questioned again.

"Very green," she panted.

He looked down at her thong and saw it was soaked. "You appear to enjoy the nipple clamps."

"I do," she agreed as he continued to caress her breasts.

Brad trailed his fingers down the delicate chain and lightly pulled on it, causing another passionate cry to escape from her lips. "With just the right pressure, I can make it feel as if two men are sucking on your nipples at the same time. Would you like that, slave?"

Shey nodded.

He pulled on the chain in light, rhythmic movements, simulating the suction of dual lovers.

Shey whimpered in pleasure.

"You can control your own pleasure, slave," he murmured huskily, ordering her to open her mouth.

It was obvious she was expecting another kiss, but he placed the chain between her lips. "I want to watch you experiment. Find the right pressure and the angles that please you."

Brad moved away and sat down on a leather armchair to watch her.

Shey stood there unmoving for several moments, surprised to be given control in the middle of their scene. She tentatively pulled on the chain, obviously afraid of the pain she imagined it would cause.

Rubbing his hand against his jeans, Brad teased himself as he watched Shey play with the clamps for the first time. If she only knew how much it turned him on...

Soon Shey began applying more pressure, making passionate moans as she found the perfect angle.

Brad pressed hard against his cock when it started to pulse with need for release, and was barely successful in warding off an unwanted orgasm. He made his way over to her again once he'd gained control over his libido, grateful that she wore a blindfold and remained unaware of the power she had over him.

Removing the chain from her mouth, he said gruffly, "Consider these clamps a gift from me, slave. You have pleased your Master well." Brad kissed her roughly as he played with the nipple clamps, causing Shey to whimper again.

When she began to tremble in his arms with need, he pulled away.

"Please…I want you," she begged.

It would be so easy to take her—to pull Shey down to the floor and tear her panties off so he could bury his cock deep inside, but he knew it would compromise this rare connection between them.

"As a gentleman, I am required to honor the parameters of our scene, no matter how much I wish to do otherwise."

Shey groaned with unsated desire.

Her desperate cry almost broke his resolve. "Slave, I believe it's time you felt the bite of my whip."

The girl suddenly tensed, her burning desire instantly transforming into fearful excitement. "How do I do this? I mean…how…do you want me?"

Brad growled hungrily, "I want you to turn around. Lean against the frame of the door so your ass is displayed for whipping."

She turned around and nervously felt for the frame with her fingers.

"Pull your thong down to your knees, girl."

Shey made a charming sight as she wiggled the garment down, exposing a hint of her red pussy as she bent over to lean against the doorframe. She arched her back, her long, wavy copper hair cascading down it as she gripped the cold metal with white knuckles.

"I could stare at you for hours…"

"Thank you, Master."

"While I may take pleasure in looking at you, I enjoy

the whip far too much to remain idle for long. Keep your legs together and lean farther forward. I'm about to pinken that pretty ass of yours."

She giggled nervously as she followed his instructions.

Brad unfurled the whip and snapped it, grinning when he saw her flinch. "Are you feeling brave?"

She held her head up higher and said loudly, "I am, Master."

"Courageous enough to take the bite of my whip, slave?"

She hesitated for only a second before answering, "I believe so."

He chuckled. "An honest answer. I appreciate that."

Brad warmed up his arm and cracked the whip next to her ear, relishing when she cried out in surprise.

"Are you aware the room is completely soundproof? No one will hear you when you scream."

She shuddered where she stood.

"Color, slave?"

"Still green, Master."

"Remember to call out your safeword at any point. There's no shame in honoring your limit."

Shey nodded, but he could see she was shaking as she waited for the first stroke.

"You must relax if you want to feel the brilliance of my instrument."

She stopped shaking for a moment, but her fear took over again, and she began shivering even more.

Brad lowered his whip as he approached her, making low noises the way he used to when he calmed horses as a boy. Shey responded the same way a filly would, pausing and then turning slightly to his voice as her body began to visibly relax.

"There is no reason to fear my whip. Tonight I will simply teach you its unique character."

She nodded, laughing at herself. "I trust you."

"Good." He pulled back her hair to expose her delicate ear and whispered, "It's okay to fear. It is a natural response to something new and potentially harmful. The key is to transform your fear into expectation."

"Yes…" she agreed, panting as he kissed her on the earlobe before leaving a trail of light kisses down her neck.

"Remember my intent as you wait for the first stroke."

"What is your intent, Master?" she asked nervously as he moved away.

"To please you, slave."

Helping her Fly

S hey let out a nervous sigh as he moved back into position behind her.

"Relax," Brad repeated gently as he swung the whip around, slowly inching closer to her ass with each swing until finally...contact.

She let out a small squeak, then giggled at herself. "That was actually nice."

"I want you to count them out loud. They will become progressively more challenging, slave."

She swallowed hard but nodded, adding a quick "Yes, Master" afterward.

He flicked the left buttock, another light stroke that would tickle like the brushing of coarse hair on skin.

"Two," she purred, obviously enjoying the light caress of the whip.

Brad continued with gentle strokes, teasing her with them. He noticed she stuck out her ass farther, silently begging for more attention. That was when he cracked the whip over her head and she screamed, before bursting into giggles again.

"It sounds so scary."

He smiled, delivering the next stroke with more power. The startled cry that followed was quite charming.

"Color, slave?"

She took a few deep breaths before answering, "May I have another to decide?"

He gave her an equally challenging stroke on her right cheek, and she squealed again before panting out the word, "Gr...een."

"You're sure?"

She nodded her head vigorously. "It's...exhilarating."

He was pleased that the bullwhip thrilled her and started his rhythmic strokes, watching her ass redden with each carefully placed lash.

When her voice heightened in pitch as she counted out the next number, he chose to stop. Brad let her bask a moment in the glow of the sub-high the whip created. Part of his talent lay in making the session a dance of sensation and longing. He enjoyed reading his sub during play and gauging the flow of the session based on her need and experience.

He suspected Shey's enthusiasm could get her in trouble with a less-experienced Dom. It would have been easy to interpret her eagerness as an okay to let loose in a volley of demanding strokes. However, as a novice, she deserved this gentle introduction.

Brad knew it was better to leave them longing for more than to destroy a sub's newfound love of the intimidating instrument. Still...he did insist on showing her just how powerful his whip could be.

"Slave, would you like a mark?"

"Oh yes," she purred.

With a quick flick of his wrist, Brad let his whip fly, leaving not one, but two consecutive marks—each perfectly centered on her butt cheeks. She cried out at the intensity of the burn, and stood there gasping for breath.

Brad lowered his whip, placing it on the table as he made his way over and untied her blindfold, letting it fall to the floor. Wrapping one hand around her throat, he pulled Shey's head back and kissed her like a man possessed.

She met his passion with her own. The high created by edge play always made for a satisfying coupling... It would be a shame if they both had to leave the scene unfulfilled.

"Slave, may I touch you here?" he asked, his other hand hovering over her naked pussy.

"Please...Master."

He slid his fingers over her swollen outer lips and began slowly swirling his middle finger over her clit. Shey groaned deeply as he continued to kiss her. Brad decided if he could not possess her physically, then he would do so by claiming her orgasm.

"Don't resist me," he commanded.

Shey moaned in response as she pressed her back against his body and attempted to open her legs wider, her thong still at her knees.

To have this control over her—delivering pain, then orchestrating her pleasure—was the ultimate turn-on.

Brad pushed his hard cock against her, wanting Shey to know the level of his arousal as he slowly urged her orgasm.

Her whole body stiffened just before she screamed passionately as her climax washed over her. He tightened his hold around her waist to keep her from falling. Shey collapsed against him, shuddering in his arms. "I'm completely undone…"

"But I haven't finished with you yet," he growled in her ear.

Brad unceremoniously threw Shey over his shoulder, smacking her lightly on her sore ass, inciting a small squeal.

He walked over to the couch to grab a pillow before carrying her into the dining room and laying her down on the table. He gently placed the pillow under her tender buttocks after pulling her thong back up to provide Shey with a semblance of modesty, straightening her pretty bow.

"You mentioned wanting to eat in here." Shey whimpered as he took off his hat and laid it on the table before slowly lowering himself to the ground. "Well, prepare to get eaten, darlin'…"

He pushed the material of her thong to the side to take his first lick of her. Her pussy was sweet and enticing, letting him know she was a lover of pineapple. It was an enjoyable treat he hadn't expected.

Shey shook her head back and forth, moaning when her body began to quiver uncontrollably. He easily brought her to another climax with his tongue. She squeezed his head hard with her thighs as her orgasm took hold and her clit pulsed against his tongue. It was worth the slight discomfort, knowing he could elicit that kind of reaction from her.

Shey mewed softly afterward. "Oh my God…oh my God… I can't believe I came that hard. Where have you been all my life?" She rubbed her hands over her breasts and down toward her loins, purring in satisfaction.

He smiled from between her legs, stating, "I find particular satisfaction in a woman's pleasure. It's part of my attraction to BDSM."

"I always assumed the Dom would be concerned about his own needs, not mine."

"We're all different, but that's where my enjoyment lies."

She looked up at the ceiling, a blush covering her chest as she murmured, "No wonder you're so popular with the ladies…"

He picked her up and carried her out of the dining room.

"I can't," she protested, apparently thinking that he was headed toward the bedroom.

Brad chuckled as he sat down on the large leather sofa with her still cradled in his arms. "Can't what, slave? I never leave a sub without aftercare."

She snuggled against him. "Oh, *aftercare*…I've always wanted to experience that."

Brad kissed the top of her copper head. "You were courageous tonight."

Shey looked up at him shyly. "Thank you."

He kissed her on the lips tenderly. "And it was a pleasure being your first."

Her pupils were large and luminous—a by-product of the endorphin high their play had induced.

Fuck, she is beautiful...

Brad rubbed his hand against her buttocks, purposely grazing the marks he'd left.

"Ooh..." she squeaked, squirming in his arms.

"I like that you chose to wear my marks."

She glanced down where his hand rested. "It's a shame I have nowhere to show them off."

He rubbed the area gently. "My marks were meant solely for you, Shey." Using her given name took the conversation to a more intimate level and signified the end of the scene. She responded by cuddling closer, purring when he started lightly caressing the curve of her buttocks.

"Do you think I would make a good sub, Master Anderson?"

He noticed she avoided looking him in the eyes when she asked. Brad held her tighter, feeling unusually possessive of her. "You would make a good sub for the right Dominant...but you must be more cautious next time. Asking a complete stranger to do whatever he wants with your body could get you in serious trouble."

She looked at him sheepishly. "What you don't know is that I've had a crush on you ever since I saw you on the red carpet, the night you protected Miss Bennett at the premiere of her documentary. Even though she wasn't your submissive, that protective look in your eye as you put yourself between her and the attackers was...well, it totally melted my heart."

Brad shook his head. "I didn't even realize I made the news that night."

She blushed when she admitted, "I printed out every picture of you I found on the Web. *Every* picture."

He raised an eyebrow. "Should I be worried then, Miss Allen?"

"No, I'm not a stalker," she answered with a giggle. "You have to admit you're an incredibly handsome man. I'm positive I'm not the only one with a Master Anderson shrine in her bedroom." When he continued to look at her warily, she added, "Remember, you came to *my* hotel tonight."

Brad laughed as he held Shey tight, enjoying the feel of her in his arms—a little too much—and was reluctant when it was time to let her go. He released his hold and helped Shey to her feet.

"You should really eat more. It feels like a tiny gust could blow you away."

Shey gave him an awkward smile as she slipped on her clothes, readying herself to leave.

Once she was fully dressed, Brad came up behind her and wrapped his arms around her waist, unhappy the time had finally come to say good-bye. "It's been a pleasure spending the evening with you, Miss Allen."

She leaned her head back and sighed. "I wish it didn't have to end…" She paused for a moment and then turned around in his arms, looking up at Brad with those sparkling blue eyes. "And it doesn't have to, at least not yet. I have a secret I'd love to show you."

Although it was getting late, and he knew that prolonging the inevitable was unwise, Brad smiled down at her and shrugged. "Why not?"

"Great, 'cause I'm about to show you my favorite place in the whole wide world."

Surprise

B rad threw on a shirt and his shoes before following her out the door. In the elevator Shey explained, "About six months ago I was going through an extremely rough patch in my life. I still came to work on time and put in my best effort—heck, I doubt anyone on staff had a clue how depressed I was—except for Mr. Nyte. I don't know how he knew, because I've never met the man in person, but I got a note one night at the end of my shift."

Shey dug through her purse and handed it to him to read.

Dear Miss Allen,

Life is a journey. When I lose sight of that, I visit my sanctuary. I offer it to you now. Please feel free to visit it whenever you feel the need. Your thumbprint has already been encoded, but the key included in this letter is also required to enter.

If the room is in use, the keypad will deny you

access so there is no chance of you disturbing me.

Miss Allen, your hard work and dedication to our clients have not gone unnoticed. However, your smile is missing, and I would like it to return.

Sincerely,

Mr. Nyte

Brad handed her back the note, stating, "That was a thoughtful gesture."

"I had no idea what a gift he'd given me until I saw the place. It's like a miracle—an oasis in the middle of the Nevada desert."

"Do you think he'll be upset if you share it with me?"

Shey shook her head. "Although I would prefer to ask, I have no way of contacting Mr. Nyte tonight. Since you will be leaving in the morning, I don't see the harm."

They stopped on the highest floor, but the doors didn't open until Shey pressed her thumb against the touchpad. She guided him through a series of hallways until they came to a green door.

Shey pressed her thumb against another security lock, and the door opened into a small foyer. Shey shut the door behind them and then approached the second door with a golden keyhole. She took a similarly colored key out of her purse and inserted it into the lock. She turned it, a look of excitement on her face as she said breathlessly, "Prepare to be amazed!"

The door slowly swung open, and the first thing that hit him was the clean scent of freshly cut lawn. He stepped into the darkened room and was startled to feel the floor give a little under his feet. Looking down, he looked down and saw it was covered in a carpet of living grass. As his eyes adjusted, he saw a virtual forest before him, complete with leafy trees, a running stream in the middle of the massive room, and the wide expanse of sky above them protected by a barrier of clear glass.

"It truly is an oasis," he murmured as she led him inside.

"In the daytime, the air is full of butterflies and the sound of birds chirping. It reminds me of the magical candy room in *Willy Wonka and the Chocolate Factory*. It has the same surreal quality, doesn't it?"

She guided him over to the stream and pointed at the water. He looked down and saw the outlines of giant fish swimming about.

"Even the water is teeming with life."

Shey pointed excitedly at a large fish as it swam by. "That one there I named Troy 2."

Brad stared at her in disbelief.

"But you can call him T2." Shey giggled, bumping her shoulder against him. "What can I say? I *really* love my cat."

"Apparently…"

"There are even squirrels and hummingbirds here. It's like a cornucopia of animal life in the daytime, but when all the creatures are asleep at night, the real magic begins."

She lay down on the soft grass and beckoned him to join her. Brad stretched out beside her, and they stared up at the stars together.

"In Vegas, it takes a really tall building to be able to see the stars," she explained. "I come up here instead of eating during my dinner breaks whenever I get the late shift."

"Is that why you're so thin?"

Shey turned her head toward him, frowning sadly. "I pretty much stopped eating when I found out Laura was carrying Sam's child. It was bad enough when they got married a year ago, but when *that* happened…I kind of broke inside. She was living my life, and I was stuck with nothing. No partner, no marriage, and no…baby girl."

Brad huffed. "Amy has a child as well, so I completely understand that sentiment."

Shey put her hand on his and squeezed. "It's nice to have someone who can relate. My friends told me to just get over it, but I've needed this time to mourn the life I will never have." She smiled at him. "I haven't eaten this much in a long time, though. I think I may finally be ready to move on."

"What does moving on look like for you, Shey?"

She shrugged. "Not much different, I suppose. I plan to keep working here at the Nyte and helping my parents out on the weekends. It's my lot in life, but I accept that now."

"Are your parents ill?"

"No, they're just old. I could never leave Vegas because of them. They're the only family I've got."

"No brothers or sisters?"

Shey's face crumpled. She turned her head away when she told him, "I'd rather not talk about it."

Brad grasped her chin and gently turned her back

toward him to kiss her sweet lips. "Then we won't, Shey."

He looked back up at the stars and stated, "I wish you could move to LA. I'm certain you'd love life on the beach. There's always something to do, and when the pressure gets to be too much, you can sit by the ocean and let the waves carry your troubles away."

"It sounds wonderful," she agreed wistfully.

"Too bad fate has determined our paths aren't meant to mesh. My life is in LA, and yours is here with your family."

"Yeah...to be honest, I don't think it would ever work between us anyway. I couldn't handle you training submissives every day. I know it'd make me a jealous wreck."

"Being the headmaster does make having a committed relationship harder," Brad confessed. "Not many women can wrap their heads around the fact it's simply a job for me. I don't allow emotional attachments with my students."

Shey laughed. "Well, we saw how well that worked for Sir Thane Davis."

"Ah, but Brie was the exception. He'd worked there for years without incident before she came along."

"Still...I don't think many women could handle having their man train other women to be good submissives."

Brad crossed his arms under his head and let out a long sigh. "I suppose that means I'm doomed to live alone."

"Me too..."

"Fate is a bugger."

Shey giggled. "Yes, he certainly is."

Brad growled in resignation as Shey snuggled up against him, and they both grew quiet as they gazed up at the stars. The sound of the trickling stream, along with the occasional rustling as animals moved about in the dark, enhanced the peaceful revelry.

Suddenly, the sky lit up as a brilliant trail of light shot across, causing Shey to cry out in delight. "Did you see the shooting star? Did you make a wish?"

Brad chuckled. "No, I gave up wishing on stars a long time ago."

"Well, I haven't." Shey proceeded to close her eyes and mouthed words to herself.

What she didn't know was that he'd actually made a wish as the bright light trailed across the night sky—he just wasn't willing to admit it, especially when there was no chance of it coming true.

Shortly after the shooting star, Shey's phone started ringing. She glanced at it briefly, quickly dismissing the call. "Must be a wrong number." She stared at it again and let out a low groan. "Crud, I really have to go. I just saw the time. It's already two in the morning, and my shift starts at six."

"It's that time then." Brad stood up and offered his hand to her. "We both knew it would come to this." He took one last long look at the sanctuary before leaving. "I'm glad you brought me here. I'll never forget it—or this night with you."

She smiled as she entwined her arm in his and they made their way down the hall to the elevator. Once they reached his floor, she hesitated for a moment. "I hate to say good-bye."

"You can spend the night," he offered, hoping against hope she would agree.

Tears came to her eyes when she shook her head in answer.

Brad stepped out of the elevator and nodded in understanding, tipping an imaginary hat to her. "Take care of yourself, Shey." He stood and watched as the elevator doors began to close. He *almost* thrust his hand out to stop them, but remained still. He knew the headmaster position he'd accepted precluded him from pursuing Shey further, so he allowed the doors to close and walked back to his room, sighing heavily as he unlocked the door.

Some things weren't in the cards...

He'd known that before the evening had even started. It was foolish to wish it was otherwise now.

Cayenne met him at the entrance, meowing piteously. He picked up the tiny kitten and petted her behind the ears. "Looks like it's just you and me, kid." Brad walked over to the scenic window that overlooked the flashy city below him. "As much as I wish it were otherwise, I have to face the fact that I'm unlucky in love...even in Vegas."

He placed Cayenne on the bed and started packing up his equipment. After a quick shower, he threw off the duvet and settled into the king-size bed. Cayenne climbed onto his chest and began purring happily as she kneaded his hairy chest with her paws before settling down for the night.

"At least one of us is happy," he said, chuckling to himself.

Brad set his alarm for 5:30, determined to leave at the break of dawn. The sooner he was away from this place, the sooner he could get on with his new life. He used the room's voice command to shut off the lights, and covered himself and Cayenne with a light sheet.

He was almost asleep when he heard a light knock on the door. It was so faint that he ignored it at first, thinking it was only his imagination. The second time it started up, however, he bolted out of bed. He took a look through the peephole, and a wide smile spread across his face when he saw a gorgeous crown of red hair on the other side.

"Just a moment," he called out, running to the bathroom to grab the silk robe set out for guests. He rushed to open the double doors to see her tear-stained face.

"What's wrong, Shey?" he asked, quickly ushering her inside.

"I…"

He guided her to the couch and waited for her answer. Shey smiled up at him, but her doe-like eyes filled with tears again. "I don't want to miss this chance to spend the night with you. I drove all the way home before I knew I had to turn around and come back." Her bottom lip trembled when she confessed, "The fact is, Brad, I would rather have one night with you than spend the rest of my life regretting that I walked away."

"I don't want to hurt y—"

She put her finger to his lips. "I know it can't work between us. But we have this night, and I desperately want to make love with you. I've never wanted anything or anyone as much." She lightly caressed his jawline. "I long to know the love of a good man. It will bring me solace in the days ahead, not pain. I understand what tonight is—we're simply two ships passing in the night. You would never hurt me, just as I would never hurt you."

He leaned down and claimed her lips, thinking to himself, *But you already have...*

Brad had known the moment he opened the door that his heart was lost. When he'd invited her into the room, he'd accepted the pain that was soon to follow. It was worth having this rare moment now.

"I'll hold nothing back, Shey," he warned.

She leaned in to kiss him. "I wouldn't want you to." Shey paused for a moment before taking his face in both hands and gazing deep into his eyes. "I want *all* of you, Master Brad Anderson."

He groaned lustfully, his emotions threatening to overwhelm him even as his cock grew rigid in response to her invitation. "You may live to regret those words, darlin'."

"How so?" she asked breathlessly as he swept her off her feet.

"I'm about to show you," he growled as he laid her down on the bed and his hand began inching up the material of her dress. Brad nibbled on her neck as his fingers leisurely made their way up her thigh.

A woman—especially one as inexperienced as Shey appeared to be—needed to be gradually prepared to take his girth. It was possible she might run out the door once she saw his shaft in all its intimidating glory.

But Shey was no shrinking violet. As he began to undress her, she undressed him, untying his robe and going straight for his briefs.

He put his hand on her tiny wrist. "Don't you want to savor this time together?"

"Of course, and I will, but you are a present I've been longing to unwrap."

Brad smirked as he let go and laid his head back on the pillow, allowing Shey to continue. She lowered the elastic band to expose the head of his shaft. "Oh...that *is* impressive." She teased herself by slowly baring the rest of his cock one centimeter at a time, her eyes growing bigger the lower she went. When she finally reached the base of his shaft, she let out a small gasp. "It's even bigger than I imagined."

"Ready to bolt?" he asked, only half joking.

Shey smiled hungrily. "Oh no, you've only made me more certain I made the right choice coming back tonight."

Yet again, she'd managed to surprise him.

"I must admit, I'm curious how all of that is going to fit inside of little ol' me."

"Let me show you..." he said, taking over. His mouth returned to her throat as he caressed her thighs. He pushed the material of her dress above her waist to reveal her enticing thong.

"I've resisted that bow all night," he told her, taking one end of the tie and tugging on it lightly. The satin material gave easily and fell away, revealing her red mound to him. He placed his hand on it reverently.

"Miss Allen, that is one lovely pussy you have there."

Shey blushed, trying to hide her pleased smile.

He brushed his hand over her pubic hair and was gratified when she raised her hips slightly, indicating that she wanted to be touched.

"I'm going to romance your fine pussy before I fill you with my cock," he whispered intimately.

"Oh…"

Shey closed her eyes as he began caressing her body, making her anticipate the next light touch. He took his time, intent on two things: getting her wet and relaxed enough to take his cock, and—even more important— seducing her heart.

Through his careful ministrations, Shey was soon slick with need, squirming and moaning in passionate desire. That's when he started whispering in her ear, sharing the little things he'd noticed about her during the evening, those aspects of her personality that made her unique and utterly irresistible to him.

At one point he noticed she was crying. "What is it?"

Shey looked into his eyes, her voice choked with emotion. "No one has ever said such kind things to me before."

"I'm not one to flatter, Shey. I only speak the truth." He sealed his assertion with a kiss.

"I want you, Brad… I need to feel you inside me."

Her words affected his heart as well as his body. With slow, purposeful movements, he stood up, shrugged off the robe, and removed his briefs, wanting Shey to see his naked body before he claimed her. Instead of her gaze drifting down to his chest or rock-hard shaft, though, her eyes remained transfixed on his.

It was a first for him, and made him desire her that much more. It appeared this was to be a melding of spirits, not just the physical connection of a man and a woman sleeping together for the first time.

Brad returned to the bed and finished undressing her, taking his time even though he longed to bury his cock inside her.

Anticipation is everything.

He positioned himself between her legs and pressed the head of his cock against her wet opening. Brad remained still, wanting to prolong the moment before penetration.

"Don't be afraid," she told him.

That amused Brad. "I'm savoring the moment, darlin'. This man likes to take his time when he makes love to a woman."

She smiled up at him, her eyes radiant with passion and tenderness.

He slowly pushed his cock into her, their eyes locked on each other. He took Shey a little at a time, reveling in the tight embrace of her body.

She received him, never once flinching or crying out as he penetrated her with his large shaft. When the base of his cock finally pressed against her coppery pubic hair, he groaned deeply.

"There is nothing more beautiful," he confessed, gazing down on the point where their bodies met.

Shey lifted her head to look. "Oh my God, that's sexy."

"You've taken my shaft, Shey, but you said you

wanted all of me."

She nodded eagerly, laying her head back on the pillow. "Give it to me."

He pushed the head of his cock even farther inside her, causing Shey to moan. He looked down, seeing the slight bulge of her stomach caused by his deep penetration. It excited him knowing her body had taken his fullness, but he wanted more. "Do you feel how deep I am?"

"Yes...I'm aware of nothing else."

"Being a Dominant causes many men to forget how to make love to a woman—I am not one of those men." He leaned down and kissed her as he started thrusting.

Shey stiffened for a moment, but her body soon relaxed as he began playing with her breasts while stroking her with his cock. The gentle manipulation of his hands and mouth incited a primal response within her, preparing her body to receive what was coming.

When he felt she was ready, he gave her his full thrust. She cried out, and then smiled to herself, apparently liking the challenge of his shaft. "Again," she begged.

But Brad's intent was not simply to fuck her well. "Look at me, Shey."

She gazed up at him with those magnetic blue eyes as he began to make slow, beautiful love to her body. She'd wanted all of him, so he gave her more than his cock, more than his skill as a Dom—that night, he gave Shey his heart.

Lying in his arms afterward, Shey sighed in contentment. "This was the best night of my life."

"No regrets?" he asked as he kissed her.

"No, it was everything I hoped for."

"And tomorrow?"

She looked up at him. "Tomorrow and every day I will look back on tonight and know that I was loved."

He held her tighter. "A life without regret is a precious thing."

She leisurely glanced at the clock on the nightstand. "It's five in the morning…"

"Time to make the donuts."

She giggled, cuddling closer. "Will you be heading out soon?"

"Yes."

Shey gave him a series of kisses across his chest. "These are for good luck," she murmured playfully.

"Much appreciated, darlin'."

Looking at the clock again, she finally slipped out of bed. "I need to make a quick trip home. It doesn't look good to come into work all disheveled and smelling like good sex."

"Best perfume I know."

She laughed. "While I may agree, my manager won't." Moving quickly, she got dressed but seemed reluctant to leave.

Brad got out of bed and walked over to her, understanding her hesitance. He leaned down and scooped up his hat, placing it squarely on her head. "Why don't you keep this?"

"It's yours," she protested.

"Exactly."

She touched the brim of the hat tenderly. "I will cherish it, Brad."

Shey paused for a moment, and then wiggled out of her thong, handing it to him. "An even exchange."

He took her offering and brought it to up to his lips, kissing the material while looking into her eyes. "Thank you."

The time had come to say their final good-byes, so he put his hand on the small of her back as he guided her to the door. "I have just one piece of advice before you go—you can take it or leave it."

She turned to face him. "Please, I'm all ears."

"Why don't you talk to your parents? I have a feeling they would prefer to see their daughter happy— wherever that might take you."

Shey was about to protest, but then thought better of it. "I will take that under consideration."

"Any advice for me?" he asked with a disarming grin.

"Don't change, Brad. Not for anyone."

He closed his eyes for a moment, the pain and em- barrassment of his breakup with Amy pricking at his conscience.

"Brad…"

Shey looked as if she had more to say but was reluc- tant to voice it.

"Go on."

"Maybe your attraction to Amy was misplaced. It's

possible you mistook her for the woman you were really meant to spend your life with."

"It's possible…"

"Not that I'm suggesting it's me or anything," she quickly amended. "We've already discussed that. I… I just don't think you should regret that breakup. I feel certain you were destined for someone else."

"I'll keep that in mind."

"Good," she said with a curt nod. "Well, this is it, then."

"This is it," he agreed, leaning in for a kiss.

She lifted her head, gazing into his eyes as their lips touched.

God, he didn't want to let her go… "If you ever make it to LA, you should look me up," he said, scribbling down his new home address and handing it to her before he opened the door.

Shey only smiled, trying desperately not to cry.

"One more kiss," he insisted, wanting to taste those lips one last time. She melted in his arms, needing the connection as much as he did.

Damn, I can taste the next fifty years of my life on those lips.

Brad nodded as she turned to leave, keeping his smile intact as he watched Shey walk out the door and out of his life…

Moving On

B rad pulled away from Vegas in his black Chevy, forcing himself *not* to look back in the rearview mirror. No reason to dwell on Shey. It had been a spectacular one-night encounter—which was all it was ever meant to be.

Cayenne was sitting in the passenger seat ready to go. Brad reached over and scratched the top of her head. "You ready for the craziness of Cali, little lady?"

She tilted her head sideways to guide his fingers under her chin, purring loudly for him.

Brad chuckled upon hearing her audible joy, but was forced to put both hands on the wheel to avoid a dead tabby cat in the road.

"Damn...not everyone is lucky in this life," he murmured, staring intently at the endless desert road in front of him. "I guess all we can do is keep moving forward and appreciate what we have." He scratched her head again, smiling down at the kitten.

Cayenne moved over to him and settled in his lap. He appreciated her companionship and mentally thanked

Brie again for gifting the kitten to him. He wondered how the newlyweds were doing.

He'd seen a few honeymoon pictures floating around the internet, but hadn't heard from either Thane or Brie personally since Italy. It would be good to reconnect with them, once he had the Training Center running the way he envisioned and his new house in order.

Ah, The Submissive Training Center…

Who would have guessed he'd be the one to take over the headmaster position for the illustrious school? When he hadn't been given the job the night Thane stepped down, he'd assumed the opportunity was lost to him forever—which was why he'd returned to Colorado and built The Denver Academy.

But fate was a wily mistress, leaving him responsible for *two* Training Centers: one as headmaster and the other as CEO.

Really, when he looked back on his life, he'd done pretty damn well for himself.

Brad looked down and sighed heavily as he petted Cayenne's tiny frame.

Why isn't it enough?

He shook his head, disgusted with himself. He had no reason to complain. Life had been more than fair— good friends, financial success, a huge cock, and an unlimited number of women to play with. Wasn't that every man's fantasy?

"Don't let me wallow in self-pity, Cayenne. If you find me leaning that way, just bite me. I'll take the hint."

She looked up at him and meowed, apparently agreeing to his request.

"Excellent."

Brad set his mind on the few changes he wanted to make at The Center. It was important not to mess too much with a system that was currently working, but still…it needed a little tweaking to help it thrive in an ever-changing world.

"Hell, I was made for this job," he said proudly. His business background, along with his recent experience creating a replica of the school in Denver, made him the ideal candidate—especially since he personally knew the staff and got along well with them.

I'm just following my destiny…

Fate seemed to be laughing at him when the traffic came to a standstill just as he was entering LA's city border. Rather than brood about it, and not a man to waste time, Brad used the irritation as an opportunity to call Marquis Gray with his truck's hands-free system.

After several rings, the trainer picked up and immediately asked, "Master Anderson, how may I assist you?"

"I need to run a few ideas by you concerning the Training Center and wondered if you were up for a visit tonight."

"Are you already settled in LA?"

He snorted. "No, I'm currently sitting in a traffic jam, but figured I should hit the ground running with the next session starting next week. Any chance we can meet tonight to discuss things?"

"I admire your work ethic, and will let Celestia know to expect you for dinner. We'll start off with a home-cooked meal before we begin."

"No reason to go to any trouble."

"Nonsense," Marquis insisted. "It's the least we can do to welcome the new Headmaster."

Brad hung up, suddenly curious if Marquis had been unhappy at not being chosen for the position himself. Making a mental note, he decided to ask the man at dinner.

Best to know now where Marquis stood on the matter.

Brad sighed in relief when he finally pulled up to his new place just as the sun was setting. It was not a looker compared to his Denver home—not by a long shot. The 1960s structure had been well maintained, but definitely had that distinctive architecture people either loved or hated. As far as he was concerned, Brad rather liked it.

The deciding factor had been its proximity to The Center. Now that he was in charge of the school, he wanted to be right in the mix of things. He'd grown to like the convenience in Denver, and wasn't willing to sacrifice that kind of control now that he was living in LA.

Baron had actually been the one to find the home and called to caution him before Brad made the final purchase. "Just a reminder, it's a diverse neighborhood."

"I prefer diversity, keeps things interesting."

"Then you should like it well enough. The neighborhood is older, and is known for its wide range of ethnic joints, some of the best in LA actually. You'll never tire of the cuisine, I guarantee it."

"Then I'll have to eat out more often."

"Let me know once you're settled. I'd be happy to take you around and introduce you to my friends who live in the area."

"Does it have a night life?"

Baron laughed. "Naturally. Things don't really start humming until after ten."

"I suggest we hang out after training at The Center one night. No reason to put off a good time."

A low chuckle met his proposal. "I like your way of thinking, Headmaster. Glad to be working with you again."

"Grateful to have you on the panel, Baron. With you and Marquis, I'm guaranteed to have a successful first session, but I'm not thrilled about having to pick a suitable Domme so late in the game."

"Yes, it's a shame Lady Crimson had to step down. I heard she did well as Ms. Clark's replacement."

"Yeah, I'm not happy," Brad grumbled in irritation. "Having babies is inconvenient for everyone."

"Not a fan of children, I take it?" Baron chuckled.

"I'll confess that children are like little aliens to me."

"You do realize you were a child once."

"My parents are far more patient than I am, Baron."

"Hmm...I find that hard to believe," Baron stated with amusement. "You're quite the patient man—willing to wait weeks for the perfect prank to play out."

Brad snorted. "Okay, okay...I'll admit there are some things I have patience for, but babies aren't one of them."

"Duly noted."

"I'll see you in LA soon."

"Looking forward to it, Headmaster."

When Brad opened the door to his new home, he found a gift basket waiting for him on the counter.

It was from Baron.

In it were several wines, dried meats and cheeses, nuts and berries, and a pair of baby booties. Brad had to laugh as he picked up the unwanted item and tossed it outside.

Wasting little time, he took a bath—in no mood to search through the many boxes to find his shower curtain. Unfortunately, it took longer than he wanted, and Brad arrived at Marquis Gray's ten minutes late.

He immediately apologized when Marquis opened the door. "Please let Celestia know I'm heartily sorry for being late."

Marquis gestured him inside. "She's just finishing up. It's no problem at all."

Brad glanced at the dinner table and saw everything was already set out. Celestia came from the kitchen with a welcoming smile on her face. "What a pleasure to see you again, Master Anderson. Can I get you a drink? You must be exhausted from driving. Master said you were caught up in traffic because of the multi-car pileup on 95."

"Thank you kindly, Celestia. A whiskey straight up

would be much appreciated."

The sub bowed her head and went to get his drink while Marquis guided him to the table. "A shot of whiskey and a good meal should settle your nerves."

"Do you mind if I am blunt with you, Gray?" Brad asked, sitting down opposite Marquis.

"Actually, I prefer it."

"How do you feel about not being chosen as head-master for the school?"

Marquis smiled as Celestia handed over the drink to Brad before taking the seat next to Marquis.

"I turned the position down, Master Anderson. It was *I* who recommended you for the job after speaking with Sir Davis about it."

Brad took a draught of the smooth whiskey, trying to quell the expression of surprise on his face. "What made you think to consider me since I was passed by the first time?"

Marquis's eyes shone with interest as he leaned forward. "I appreciate your forward thinking. It's what's needed for The Center."

"I'm glad to hear you say that. Naturally, I respect the school's history and its unparalleled curriculum, but I've noticed a few areas that could use improvement."

Marquis sat back, nodding his head. "Agreed. I'm sure your first order of business is to find a replacement for Lady Crimson."

"Yes, I was upset when I heard she stepped down."

Marquis inclined his head. "Unfortunate, but it is for a happy occasion."

Brad bit back his retort.

Celestia handed Brad a dish of fresh vegetables. "We're so excited for her. She's tried for years to conceive."

"While I agree it's good news for her," Brad stated reluctantly, "it does leave us scrambling for a suitable replacement just before the next session starts."

"Do you know who you would like to offer the position to?" Marquis asked.

"I do. Been contemplating it the whole drive down from Denver, but I wanted to run it by you first."

"Certainly."

"I was thinking of asking Mistress Lou to join the team. She's been a vital part of The Training Center for years."

Marquis frowned. "While I approve of your choice, you should know that Mistress Lou has turned down the position before."

"Any particular reason why?"

"Time commitment. It's the reason she prefers to help when needed, rather than a full-time trainer."

"Hmm…" Brad knew he wanted the skilled Domme on his team, but it seemed he'd have to convince her it would be worth the time investment. "You *do* agree she's a good choice, though."

"The best, if you can get her to commit."

"Mistress Lou is highly respected," Celestia confirmed, "with Dominants and submissives alike."

"Then I will find a way to persuade her," Brad declared, dishing himself a huge portion of roast beef and potatoes.

Celestia blushed when he took a bite and smiled approvingly at her. "It's good to be back in LA, damn it."

With his friends surrounding him and no emotional baggage weighing him down, Brad felt certain he could flourish in this place.

Before he did any more work, he knew he seriously needed to visit The Haven. The tension in his body required release, and what better place to do that than at the club? It had been a long time since he'd visited the place, and his hand was twitching to acclimate a new sub to his bullwhip.

Brad had to wait in line to get in, and was shocked at the number of people inside. Gone were the days of intimate groups and casual encounters. The club was now a main destination for LA residents and out-of-towners looking for some kink. It made for a hectic atmosphere, but Brad kind of liked it. The energy was exhilarating and had his body humming for an intimate interaction.

Moving up to the bar, Brad ordered a whiskey. While waiting, he glanced around the crowded place in search of a suitable partner.

He was surprised to see a familiar face when Boa sat down beside him. "I was told you were heading back to LA."

Brad shook the submissive's hand firmly, pleased at the timely encounter. "Back and ready to begin the newest training session. By the way, is your Mistress around?"

"Sorry, Mistress Lou is burning the midnight oil tonight. She insisted I come since we normally play at The Haven at this time."

Brad was not pleased to hear that Mistress Lou was working late. It did not bode well for the position he wanted to offer her. "Boa, do you think your Mistress would have time to meet with me, say tomorrow?"

"Mistress insists on having her lunches free of work commitments. I'm certain she would enjoy seeing you again, Master Anderson."

"Good. I'll text her now," Brad told him, pulling out his phone.

"May I ask who you are scening with tonight?" Boa inquired while Brad typed.

"Haven't found a subbie yet, but I'm itching to let my bullwhip fly tonight. The owner set me up with an alcove, which will be available in a few minutes, but I need to procure a partner or forfeit the reservation."

Boa raised an eyebrow. "Ever consider scening with a male?"

Brad leaned his back against the bar as he studied Boa. "Can't say that I have."

The submissive picked up his mug of beer and casually took a drink.

Although Brad wasn't interested in males as sexual partners, he could see the allure of testing his bullwhip on a male submissive. It might prove educational for both the Dominant and sub. Before he could respond to Boa's request, however, Brad felt a light tapping on his shoulder.

"Pardon me, are you Brad Anderson?"

He looked down to see a small woman who looked to be the same age as he. He grinned, and stated, "Why I am, miss. Who's asking?"

She burst into a huge smile. "It's me—glee."

He titled his head, studying her more closely. "Name rings a bell…"

"We met at the old warehouse, way back when you, Sir Davis, and Rytsar were going to college."

"Oh, yes…I remember you, glee," he said, his grin growing bigger. "You're the one who helped introduce Thane to the lifestyle."

"I did have the pleasure of being Sir Davis's first," she replied with a slight blush.

"How has life treated you since?" Brad asked, noting that glee wore neither a collar nor a wedding band.

"I've traveled the world," glee told him, her eyes twinkling with excitement. "I've been to forty-two different countries and been under the rule of over twenty Doms during my travels. An experience of a lifetime."

"Wow," Brad stated. "I'm impressed."

"How is Sir Davis, by the way? Do you two still keep in touch?"

Brad chuckled. "Thane remains a good friend of mine, and even helped to get the job I have now."

She leaned slightly closer, showing interest without being too bold. "What do you do, Brad?"

"I'm Headmaster of The Submissive Training Center."

She looked positively shocked. "You're the Headmaster?" Glee immediately dropped to her knees to bow before him. "This is such an honor. What...what should I call you?"

"You can call me Master Anderson, and there's no need to bow. I'm not official yet. Don't start until the beginning of next week."

Glee looked at him with new interest. "How was Sir Davis involved in getting you the coveted position?"

"He used to be the Headmaster of the school."

Glee's eyes widened. "No! I've heard about The Submissive Training Center for years, but never realized who actually headed it." She shook her head. "To think I was the Headmaster's first..." She looked at Brad again and giggled. "Sir Davis was definitely different from the others."

"Apparently, you made quite the impression on him as well," Brad replied with a wink.

Glee glanced around excitedly. "Is he here now?"

"No, he's off with his new wife exploring the world like you."

"So he jumped ship and went vanilla, did he?"

"Not exactly. Brie is also his submissive."

"Ah..."

Being that glee seemed unattached, Brad asked, "Are you partnered with anyone tonight?"

"No, just came in for a quick visit before I head off to New Zealand."

"Jet-setter glee."

She giggled. "It's true, I can't get enough of traveling. Staying in one place makes me all antsy."

"Would you be interested in spending a session with

me and my bullwhip as a proper send-off?"

Her hands went to her mouth as she tried to cover her blossoming smile. "Please, Master Anderson."

"Excellent. I have an alcove reserved over there," he said. "Why don't we take a stroll to it while you tell me more about your travels?"

Brad finished his whiskey and leaned over to Boa before leaving. "We'll talk more another day."

Boa nodded, holding up his beer. "Appreciate the consideration, Master Anderson."

Brad placed his hand on glee's back to announce to others that she was taken for the evening. Without a collar, she was considered fresh pickin's, and Brad was not interested in fending off other Doms.

Despite her years, glee still held the same fire in her eyes and that youthful smile he remembered.

"I can't believe I'm about to scene with the Headmaster of The Submissive Training Center," she gushed.

"I'm glad it pleases you. I'll admit I am looking forward to it as well," he said lustfully, already imagining the lovely red marks on glee's back and her squeals of pleasure as he bent her over and found out just how much of him she could take.

Glee was in the middle of telling him about her travels in Korea, when Brad spied a disturbance several yards from them, just beyond the river of people milling past. He narrowed his eyes, an instinctual need to protect overpowering his senses.

"Excuse me for a moment," he told her before he made his way through the crowd, both submissives and Dominants standing back to make a clear path for him.

He headed straight toward the perpetrators, who were circling a curly-haired brunette with hungry looks on their faces. The woman wore a frightened expression, alerting Brad to the fact that she was way over her head with these three.

"What seems to be the problem?" he asked her directly.

One of the Dom wannabes answered for the woman. "Nothing's wrong here, bub. We're just admiring the merchandise and deciding who gets the prize."

"Strange… You *do* realize this is The Haven and not some sleazy bar."

"Fuck off," the one with stringy hair told him.

The people surrounding them hushed. No one spoke to the Headmaster that way.

Brad snapped his fingers and the owner of The Haven nodded, making his way through the sea of people to join him.

While Brad waited, he asked the three, "What are your names?"

"Why the hell would we tell you that?" the portly one of the group scoffed.

"Why wouldn't you?" Brad countered. "I'm Master Anderson, a member of the community here. And you are?"

The man didn't say anything.

"Well, I'm the Duke of Earl," the stringy-haired individual replied sarcastically.

Brad raised an eyebrow. Before the man could even react, Brad grabbed his arm and twisted it behind his back, effectively immobilizing the man.

"Get your fucking hands off me!" he cried, glaring at his friends to help.

"Watch your language in front of the lady," Brad commanded.

The two other men puffed up their chests, posturing themselves as if they wanted to fight, but neither made a move toward Brad.

"What are your names?" Brad demanded again.

"Not important," the first man sputtered, glancing at the exit as if he was ready to bolt.

"What's going on here, Headmaster Anderson?" the club owner asked as he approached.

"These men were harassing one of the submissives." He huffed when he added, "And they refuse to give me their names." He pulled up on the arm of the man he still held, causing a piteous yelp, and added in a mocking tone, "Except for the Duke of Earl here."

Addressing his two companions, Brad said, "Hand the owner your driver's licenses, along with your buddy's."

"There's no way we're doing that," the pudgy one snapped.

"You're not leaving here until you do," the club owner informed them.

The men looked around nervously when the Doms and Dommes in the crowd began encircling the three in a wall of dominant force.

The portly man looked around nervously and was the first to break under pressure. He handed over his license and dug the wallet out of the "Duke's" back pocket while Brad continued to hold on to the whiny man. The last wannabe realized there was no point in further resistance and offered over his as well.

After the owner had recorded their names, he told them, "You will not be allowed back into my club. We expect every person to behave in a respectful manner at all times." He looked around the crowded place for emphasis. "We want everyone here to have a pleasant experience. Anyone who disrupts that has no business at The Haven."

"This place is whacked," the stringy-haired man complained angrily, struggling in Brad's arms.

Brad leaned down and told him, "Duke, I know this prince who has a thing for naughty little boys. Want me to give him your number?"

"Get away from me, man!" he cried, struggling unsuccessfully to break away.

The other two sheepishly took their licenses back and were unceremoniously hauled off. Brad personally escorted the Duke of Earl out himself.

"Just say the word, and I'll sic that prince on your little duke ass," Brad joked when he finally released the man.

"I don't need this shit," he grumbled.

Brad watched the three men slink off to their car. Once he confirmed they had left the premises, he headed back into the club and found the thankful brunette waiting for him.

He immediately apologized for the treatment she'd received. "Normally people know how to conduct themselves at The Haven. You should never have to put up with disrespect—from anyone."

She looked him up and down, a look of delight on her face. "Who is this hero before my eyes?"

"Simply a Dom who doesn't condone mistreatment of submissives."

"I'm not really a submissive," she confessed, blushing. "I mean, I want to be, but I've never really had the chance and I haven't found a Dom to train me yet."

"What's your name?" he asked.

"Brandi."

Brad grinned as he pulled out his wallet and handed her a business card. "Brandi, if you're serious, you might want to consider applying."

She stared at The Submissive Training Center card in her hand, her eyes sparkling with delight when she looked up at him. "I'll definitely look into it."

Brad waved glee over to him and placed his hand on the small of her back once she arrived. "Excuse us, Brandi. I have an appointment I must keep."

"Of course," she said, tucking the card in her purse. "Thanks again for the help."

"I hope you'll consider the school. I think you would find it...inspiring."

He looked down at glee and said in a husky voice, "Shall we?"

"Please, Headmaster Anderson."

Brad was disappointed to find that the alcove was now occupied by a couple, his time having already passed. "I'm sorry, glee. This was not how I envisioned our night would go."

She squeezed his arm. "I don't mind. If more Doms stood up when they saw that kind of behavior, the world would be a much safer place."

"Most people don't want to get involved, and new-bies like her don't know what's acceptable and what's not."

"Which makes what you do at The Center so im-portant," glee stated proudly.

Brad looked around, not as enthusiastic about the crowds as he had been at first. "What would you say if I offered to scene with you at the Training Center? I'd take you to my place, but it's littered with boxes."

"The idea of that sounds divine to me, Master An-derson."

Brad called Marquis Gray on the phone before he began the scene, wanting to inform the longtime trainer of his intent so there would be no misunderstandings or hard feelings later.

"You don't need my permission," Marquis stated.

"No, but I want to maintain your trust and respect."

"Will this submissive be a student at the school at a later date?"

"No, glee is an experienced sub with no need for our classes."

"Then by all means, enjoy the equipment The Center provides. It's one of the perks of being a trainer here. Just remember to turn off the camera before beginning and turn it back on before you leave. The cameras are meant solely for training purposes."

"Appreciate the advice. Have a good evening, Gray."

"Before I let you go, any word on Lady Crimson's replacement?"

"I have an appointment with Mistress Lou tomorrow."

"I'm impressed. If you convince her to join the panel, I'll take my hat off to you."

Brad laughed. "I'll get you a hat then."

"Have a good evening, Master Anderson."

After hanging up, Brad slipped the phone in his pocket and walked over to turn off the camera in the far corner before returning to glee, who was patiently waiting for him.

Brad placed his hand on her head and said formally, "Stand and serve your Master."

The naked submissive stood up with practiced grace. He stared at her body appreciatively. Glee was a fine specimen of a woman—her feminine form in full bloom at the age of thirty-five—full of the confidence that time and experience created, with permanent marks that attested to her joy in submission. Yet, glee still maintained that infectious excitement that made her spirit inviting. Although Brad preferred the "wild ones", he could see settling down with such a woman…

"Are you ready to experience the intimacy of my whip, glee?"

"It would be my honor, Master."

"Then stand on the X."

First Day of Class

B rad was only given twenty minutes with Mistress Lou at lunch. The tense expression on her face as she approached his table made Brad apprehensive. If she was this stressed now, how could he possibly convince her to add on more by taking the position of trainer at The Center?

He held out his hand, impressed by the woman's firm grip. There was no doubt, Mistress Lou was a formidable businesswoman who could not be manipulated by flattery, so he laid his cards out on the table for her.

"As you may have heard, Lady Crimson has left her post at the Training Center. Now that I'm Headmaster, I need to find a Domme worthy to join me on the panel." He inclined his head towards her. "Naturally you were the first person who came to my mind."

He could see she was getting ready to tell him all the reasons she couldn't, but he stopped her by addressing them himself. "I know you put in far too many hours at your job. I also appreciate that you're the Mistress of several submissives who need time and attention. However, I have the perfect solution."

He grinned inwardly when Mistress Lou gave him an irritated look reserved for pushy salesmen.

"Now, Mistress Lou, if you are a trainer at the school you will have the opportunity to relieve the stress of your day job by physically working with our students every night during the six-week course. You can include your submissives in the Dominant training sessions as well, thereby giving them the attention they need while, at the same time, benefitting those who require their experienced submission to learn and grow." He leaned toward her when he gave his closing line, "Just think that for six weeks every few months, you will have the opportunity to change lives while still keeping those things most important to you a priority."

Mistress Lou stared at him, her expression stoic. She seemed quite unaffected by his heartfelt pitch.

Brad leaned back in his chair. That's all he had—and it hadn't been enough, he could tell it by the look in her eye.

"My submissive Boa said he spoke with you last night."

Seeing an unexpected lead-in, Brad set his elbows on the table and nodded.

"There are few men I would be interested in Boa scening with. You happen to be one of them." Her eyes sparkled when she added, "I know it's not your inclination to dominate males with your whip, but I quite like the idea of observing you two together."

Seeing this golden opportunity set before him, Brad

wanted to jump in without hesitation, but played hard to get. "As you said, male submissives are *not* my thing."

She pursed her lips. "I'm not interested in you fucking him, Master Anderson. Simply exposing him to the force of your whip. Witnessing the power exchange between two well-endowed men, confident in their opposing roles, would be an extraordinary experience."

He raised an eyebrow, saying nothing.

"The idea intrigues me enough that I would agree to become a trainer for the reasons you stated, as long as you sweeten the pot by agreeing to scene with Boa at The Haven."

"At The Haven, huh?"

Her thin red lips curled into a smile. "I know I am not the only one who would enjoy the exchange."

"One session with Boa is enough to convince you to join me on the panel?"

"It is."

Brad couldn't believe his luck.

"Do we have a deal?" she asked.

Brad immediately stuck out his hand to shake on the deal before she could change her mind. "Naturally, Mistress Lou."

"Good." She let go of his hand and picked up her fork, taking a small bite of her salad. "I'd already determined I would agree to your offer because I wish to work with you. However, the chance to secure a scene for my beloved sub was too good to pass up."

Brad chuckled, feeling only admiration. "So you set me up, Mistress Lou?"

"No, I simply negotiated an arrangement that was

pleasing to both parties."

He held up his glass of water and nodded to her. "Welcome to the team."

She stated in a formal voice, "It will be a pleasure to serve the community with you." The Mistress looked at her watch and abruptly stood up. "And now I must leave. It has been a pleasure conducting business with you today."

Brad watched her walk away, feeling extremely satisfied knowing his team was now complete. With Marquis, Baron, and Mistress Lou heading the panel beside him, this session of students would be well served.

He couldn't wait to begin.

Brad was in for a shock when he got a call from Brie a few nights later. She suggested he meet with the two of them at a bar. It seemed the newlyweds, who'd just returned from their honeymoon, were desperate for his company—and he couldn't have been more pleased.

Damn, today's my lucky day, he thought as he jumped in his truck.

Any excuse not to stare at his numerous boxes was a good one, but getting to hang with Thane and Brie was an unexpected bonus.

When he found out the reason for the impromptu gathering, however, he was stunned.

Completely stunned.

At first, Brad had assumed the couple was pulling an

elaborate joke on him in payment for all the ones he'd played on them. It was a huge letdown when he finally realized they were serious.

Brie and Thane were having a child, and now nothing would be the same. He left the bar smiling and waving at Brie as he drove off, but as soon as he turned the corner he bellowed, "Shit, shit, shit!"

First Amy popped out a kid—killing any chances with her. Then Lady Crimson had resigned from The Center after getting knocked up. And now Thane and Brie were expecting one of those smelly creatures.

Babies were nothing but bad luck.

Brad returned to his home feeling utterly defeated. When Cayenne jumped up on his shoulder, he scratched her furry chin, stating, "I need to look into getting you spayed, little lady. I'm not about to go through this with you too."

She mewed, rubbing herself against him.

Brad retreated to his small backyard and settled down on the old folding chair the previous owners had left behind. He looked over the neglected garden with concern, knowing action was needed.

With a determined sigh, he stood up and ripped off his shirt, heading for the farthest corner of the lot. He couldn't stop people from having babies, but he could damn well care for the abandoned plants in his yard.

Brad talked to them while he worked, attracting the attention of his next-door neighbor.

"Young man, can you help me?"

Brad stood up and looked over their shared three-foot fence. A tiny old woman who looked to be about ninety smiled back at him. Her wrinkled skin was dark, making her enthusiastic smile that much more bright and engaging.

Her eyes drifted down from his face to his chest, and she stared with the same lustful interest as women three-fourths her age. "Oh my…" she murmured.

Rather than cover up, he flexed his chest muscles and put his hands to his waist in a Superman pose. "How can I help you, miss?"

"I think my dog lost one of his balls on your side of the fence."

Brad looked down the length of the fence and saw a green tennis ball. He walked over and picked it up, handing it to the old woman with a grin.

"Thank you, young man."

"My name is Brad, I just moved in. What's your name?"

The woman tilted her head, smiling flirtatiously. "You can call me Miss Em."

He held out his hand to her over the fence. "It's a pleasure to meet you, Miss Em."

"Likewise, Mr. Brad." She stared at his chest unabashedly. "What brings you to LA?"

"A new job."

"Modeling?" she guessed.

Brad laughed, shaking his head. "No, I'm headmaster of a school. On the weekends, however, I prefer to garden." He looked around his sad little plot of land. "It looks like I have my work cut out for me."

"Yes, George and Enid weren't much into their yard. He was a carpenter, not a plant person, and she liked bingo far too much to waste time in the backyard."

Brad clapped his hands together. "Well, I'm a man who is up for a challenge."

Miss Em glanced down at his crotch, stating, "I bet you are, Mr. Brad." She looked up to meet his gaze. "I appreciate a man who can cultivate good neighbor relations. I think you will be a mighty fine fit here."

He took her hand and kissed it gallantly. "I look forward to many fine weekends spent out in the backyard."

"As do I," she replied with a twinkle in her eye.

"Unfortunately, Miss Em, I must excuse myself if I'm to make any progress tonight."

"By all means, Mr. Brad. I know it's late, but I'll go make you some lemonade and cookies." The old woman hurried into her home, giggling like a young girl.

"Maybe LA won't be so bad after all," he snorted to himself, grabbing a huge weed and yanking hard on it—thinking of Brie as he did so.

The first day of Submissive Training under his leadership had finally arrived. It had demanded a lot out of Brad to be prepared for this day, but watching the excitement of the students as they entered the building for their first day made it worth it to him.

He watched them unseen as they came through the doors, noting the way they walked and the manner in which they interacted with the receptionist, Rachael, at the desk.

Brad learned a lot by simply observing them when they didn't know they were being watched. He could already tell which girl was going to be a handful by the way she sauntered in, giving Rachael attitude before heading over to the elevator. It would be interesting to see if she lasted the night.

Brad chuckled to himself when he headed down the elevator, once all the submissives had been accounted for. One had straggled in ten minutes late, her outfit a disheveled mess. Another pupil he worried might not make the cut tonight.

He walked past Mr. Gallant's class and heard the teacher's commanding voice as he explained the levels of submission. Brad grinned to himself, knowing how much these girls would be challenged this evening.

Brad took his place at the table with the rest of the panel. "All the students are here," he told them.

Marquis pulled out a yellow pad of paper and proceeded to write down each submissive's name.

"Not giving up on the old pencil and paper, Gray?" he asked.

Marquis gave him a slight grin. "While I find a tablet more efficient, I still enjoy the feel of a pencil in my hand. It's also an effective visual for the students. When they see me writing something down, they assume they've screwed up and try even harder."

"Always the crafty one, aren't you?" Brad looked down at his tablet for a moment and asked, "You got another one on hand?"

Marquis nodded. He pulled out another pad from his briefcase and handed it to Brad along with a freshly sharpened pencil.

"What's more intimidating than two trainers scribbling on their pads?"

"Three," Baron answered. "Got a spare for me, Marquis?"

"I always come prepared," Marquis replied. He fished out a third and gave it to Baron.

Mistress Lou shook her head when Marquis offered to get her one from his office. "I simply cannot take the time to transfer my notes from paper to tablet."

Brad agreed. "We understand your time is limited, Mistress Lou. It will help you stand out and give the students something to wonder abou—"

Rachael came running in, a stricken look on her face. "Headmaster Anderson, something is wrong with one of the students. She's making odd sounds and we can't get her to speak."

Brad frowned. "Where is she?"

"She's been transferred to the trainer's lounge."

"Damn, what a way to start the new session." Taking charge, Brad ordered, "Rachael, call an ambulance right now. I'm not taking any chances with our students."

The trainers rushed behind him as Brad ran in a full sprint to see what was wrong. He burst through the door and blurted, "Oh, bloody hell…" when he saw what was waiting for him.

The others came running in after him, laughing.

Cayenne was sitting daintily on the sofa and meowed when she saw Brad. She jumped down and rubbed herself against his pant leg.

Brad looked at Marquis. "Was this really necessary?"

Baron chuckled. "I have to admit Rachael gave quite a commanding performance. She had me almost convinced something was wrong."

Mistress Lou stared at Brad, an arched eyebrow raised and a smile on her crimson lips.

Brad bent down and picked up Cayenne, who proceeded to climb up his arm and perch herself on his shoulder. "Well...you got me good," he said. "Didn't see that one coming."

"We did it for two reasons," Marquis explained. "First, it was important to see how our new Headmaster would perform under stress. You did well by the way," he said with a smirk.

Mistress Lou spoke up. "We also needed to establish our dominance in the practical joke department."

"I do feel slightly dominated right now," Brad admitted.

Baron broke out in a low chuckle.

Brad scratched the top of Cayenne's head, joining in his laughter. "You do realize that retaliation will happen when you least expect it."

"We're counting on it," Mistress Lou stated as she turned and headed out the door.

Rachael was waiting for Brad when he left the lounge. She was blushing profusely, looking deeply ashamed. "I'm sorry, Headmaster. I feel bad for scaring you like that, especially on your first day."

Brad handed her the kitten. "No reason to apologize, Rachael. It was well played."

"I'm glad you can forgive me."

He smiled, shaking his finger at her. "I actually admire you even more, Miss Rachael. However, as much as I admire your acting abilities, it will not spare you from my wrath. Prepare to get pranked."

Rachael glowed. "I look forward to it, Headmaster."

Brad returned to the panel and chuckled under his breath as he readied himself for the students. He stood up when they entered the room, each girl dressed in the required uniform of leather corset, short skirt, and those sexy high heels.

He could feel their nervous excitement as they entered, and it stirred the trainer in him. Six new students stood before the panel. How many would thrive in the six-week course and make it to the other side as educated and confident graduates?

Only time would tell.

"Take your place behind one of the ramps," he commanded in a smooth but authoritative voice.

The girls moved behind the ramps, some of them staring at them warily, while others stood at attention, looking at him with expectant faces.

"Tonight we will be weeding any wannabe submissives."

There was a shuffling of feet as his words sank in. They'd assumed up to that point that they were secured a spot after getting accepted into the school. Now they would learn the truth. Entrance was a privilege, but remaining here had to be earned.

"How can you tell who's a wannabe and who's not?" a pixie blonde with short hair asked.

"You may address me as Master Anderson. That goes for all of you," Brad ordered, looking slowly down the line, making eye contact with each student.

"Master Anderson, how can you tell?" she amended.

"We have a series of scenarios for you tonight. The four of us will be observing you to determine who should remain in the course and who should be dismissed. Understand that you can decide to leave the program at any point as well."

"Why would we do *that* when we've already paid the tuition...Master Anderson?" the girl he'd already dubbed "the attitude" questioned in a superior tone.

"Ms. Slater, restate that question so that it sounds like a question and not a disrespectful remark."

She frowned for a moment before restating the question as he had commanded.

"Ms. Slater, we are similar to Ivy League institutions. Your first few classes have been designed to eliminate the uninspired. We are only interested in training serious students, so you may choose to leave the program on your own accord or you may be asked to leave by any one of your instructors here."

"Even though we freaking paid the tuition?" she demanded.

When he didn't answer, she reworded her question. "What happens to the money we already paid, Master Anderson?"

"Should you leave for any reason, you will receive a full refund."

Ms. Slater seemed satisfied with his answer and surprised him by saying, "Thank you for clearing that up, Master Anderson."

Maybe the girl could learn humility after all.

Brad held up their application packets. "You have given us your personal lists of preferences and dislikes. We want you to be aware that the men chosen for this first practicum were picked based on your answers."

An assistant came into the room and handed each of the girls a black strip of cloth.

Brad instructed them to tie on the blindfolds and lie down on the ramps.

One of the girls looked like she was about to run. Truly, if the girl was already unsure she had no business continuing.

"Miss Rodriguez, is there a problem?"

The girl blushed profusely. "Master Anderson..."

"Yes?"

"Master Anderson, I have to pee."

Brad had to hold back his laughter. Keeping a serious expression, he told her, "All you need to do is ask permission."

"May I please go to the restroom, Master Anderson?"

"Of course, one of our assistants will show you the way. Please hurry, Miss Rodriguez. The trainers are waiting."

She gave him a quick bow and rushed out of the room.

Brad took the opportunity to stare at the rest of the students. He noted which ones shifted uncomfortably when he picked up his yellow pad and began writing. Little did they know he was simply doodling.

One girl, however, stood with her back straight, her eyes forward, and a smile that just wouldn't quit. He scribbled down her name *Miss Henderson* and wrote down *the smiler* beside it.

Once Miss Rodriguez had returned, Brad commanded once again that the girls blindfold themselves and lie down on the ramps. It was easy to feel the tension rise in the room when he nodded to the assistant and they heard the men walk in.

After each Dom had taken his place, Brad began.

"Ms. Slater, you stated in your application that you are not attracted to men with small penises."

"Yes, Master Anderson."

"Meet your partner, Sir Reed."

The expression on her face when the Dom pressed his small shaft against her vagina was priceless. Brad would be watching her closely to see if she responded to her Dom's various sexual skills or if she shut down completely because of her prejudice.

"Miss Henderson, you stated that you found short, scrawny men unattractive."

"I did, Master Anderson."

"Meet your partner, Lord Connor."

Her smile faltered for a second, until the Dom began talking to her. Brad could see her physically relax and that winning smile return. Her positive response boded well for her in the weeks to come.

Brad continued the introduction of Ms. Miller, Miss McKenzie, Ms. Grady, and Miss Rodriguez to their partners and then he sat down. The four trainers observed them closely, taking detailed notes to be shared with the students once the lesson was finished.

Surprisingly, no one ran from that first lesson but he

knew the second practicum, which was designed for each individual, would prove much more challenging.

That first night, they lost Ms. Miller. She was not keen on challenging herself with a Dom covered head to toe in tattoos. It amused Brad that what one woman found attractive, another found repulsive. It took all kinds, he mused, but her short-sightedness meant she missed out on the Dom who was an expert at her favorite tool.

Her loss…

When class ended at twelve that evening, the staff stayed behind to discuss their first impressions of the new crop of students.

"What did you think of Miss Rodriguez?" Brad asked.

Marquis replied, "A timid soul, but I saw a spark tonight. I think she will experience real growth under our care."

Baron nodded. "I found it hard not to laugh when she piped up that she had to pee."

"At least she said something," Mistress Lou said. "It would have made her session much less enjoyable had she remained silent."

Mr. Gallant smiled. "I'm glad to hear she was willing to state her need."

They all chuckled.

"Indeed," Brad agreed. "And what about Ms. Slater?"

"She has an ego that needs to be knocked down a few notches," Mistress Lou replied.

Baron shook his head. "You could tell she was arrogant from her very first words."

"I had issues with her in the classroom, myself," Mr. Gallant shared. "Every class has at least one rebellious spirit."

Marquis stated his concern. "I didn't care for the way she treated the first Dom. I think we must challenge her more. Either she will learn humility or I will personally ask her to leave."

Brad smiled, understanding his point but disagreeing. "I actually thought she would be gone by the end of the night when I first saw her. However… I now believe Ms. Slater has potential. Sometimes arrogance is a sign of ignorance. I feel strongly that is what we must free her from."

"Food for thought," Mistress Lou stated.

"What are your thoughts on Miss Henderson?"

Baron chuckled. "I like that girl. A positive attitude and a great smile."

"I concur," Mr. Gallant said. "She stands out to me as well."

"But lacking skills," Mistress Lou countered. "Frankly, I was shocked by how little she knew."

"Ah, but that's what makes her a perfect candidate for the course. There is much we can teach her and she seems eager to learn," Marquis replied.

Brad nodded. He had real hope for Miss Henderson. That brunette beauty with the long bangs, big eyes, and enticing smile…her smile would win over many a Dom. "She'll need a lesson on restraint. That smile of hers should be reserved for her Dom, and only her Dom. It could get her in trouble if she fails to understand that."

"But we must be careful not to quell her enthusiasm," Mr. Gallant cautioned.

"Never fear, Gallant. Our aim is to help our students, not harm them," Brad assured the teacher. "Now about Miss McKenzie…"

Baron nodded. "Not really a submissive, is she?"

"I don't believe so."

Mistress Lou stated, "I believe we test the level of her submissive tendencies tomorrow. Let's make it obvious to her."

Marquis graced her with a rare smile. "I couldn't agree more, Mistress Lou."

"Which leave us with Ms. Grady. Any thoughts?"

Marquis's expression became serious. "She is far too reserved. I can read most people, but I struggled with her tonight."

"She said very little in class, even when prompted," Mr. Gallant shared.

Baron expressed his main concern. "How can a Dom work with a submissive he cannot read? Although we have safewords in place, it's imperative there is an unspoken dialogue between the Dom and sub in a scene."

"She is a mystery," Mistress Lou agreed.

"We'll need to unravel what makes her tick. Of all who are left, she is the one I'm most concerned about," Brad admitted.

All four voiced their agreement.

"Still, all in all, this is quite a successful first day. Five students still under our care, and six weeks of training ahead," Brad announced proudly.

"Gentlemen, it is an honor to work with all of you." Mistress Lou gave a slight bow of her head.

"Agreed," Marquis said. "You have gathered a strong team here, Master Anderson. I see years of success ahead for The Center."

"An added bonus is that you're also entertaining," Baron said, slapping Brad on the back. "It's good to be training with you again, Headmaster."

"Let me state my gratefulness as well," Mr. Gallant added, smiling warmly at Brad.

"Tonight alone has been worth all the sacrifices it took to get here," Brad stated with sincerity.

Brad didn't get the tragic news until late that night after he'd returned home.

"Hello, is this Brad Anderson?"

"It is," he replied, alarmed by the late hour of the call.

The woman on the other end took a deep breath before telling him, "This is Judy Reynolds. Brie wanted me to call you to let you know that Thane was involved in the plane crash at LAX. He's in the ICU in critical condition."

"What? What plane crash?"

"The footage of the crash was all over the news tonight..." she mumbled. "It was terrible. There weren't many survivors."

What the hell...

"I'm really sorry to be the bearer of bad news, but you should know that the doctor says Thane is in stable condition for now."

Brad remained silent, in too much shock to speak.

Thane was his best friend—not only his old college buddy, but the man he looked up to and aspired to be like.

A world without Thane Davis in it?

Tears came to Brad's eyes at the thought. "Is there anything I can do?" he asked gruffly.

"Not right now. The seriousness of his condition does not allow for visitors."

"What about Brie?"

"She's with him and is doing well enough considering the circumstances. That girl's strong and determined."

Brad let out a long drawn-out sigh, the news of Thane's accident rocking him to the very core.

When he didn't say anything more, she added, "I'll call you if his condition changes. Since cell phones don't work in the ICU, is there a message you'd like me to pass on to Brie?"

"Tell her…" His mind was too muddled to think intelligently. "Tell her that I'm with her in spirit."

"I'll do that. Take care, Mr. Anderson."

"You do the same."

A cold chill settled over Brad after he hung up.

He headed outside in the pale moonlight to work on the garden, needing to escape from his thoughts. He wiped away the tears that refused to stop as he pulled at the weeds.

"What's wrong, Mr. Brad? I couldn't sleep and then I heard you out here."

He looked up at Miss Em. Hardly able to speak through his grief, he told her, "My best friend..." An image of Thane in a coffin came to his mind and he had to swallow down the lump that was growing in his throat. "My friend was involved in a plane crash tonight. He's at the hospital now, possibly dying."

"Oh dear..." She looked at him with empathy and held out her frail arms to him. "Let me give you a hug, young man."

Brad stepped over the small fence that divided their yards and bent down to accept the tiny woman's embrace. She patted his back and murmured, "There, there..."

As silly as it was, he found her hug comforting.

"You know what you need?" she asked.

"No, what?"

"You need some fresh brownies."

He chuckled through his tears. "You're a woman after my own heart."

"I'll go make them right now. You can come inside if you like."

Brad shook his head. "Thank you, Miss Em, but I'd prefer to stay outside and work on the garden. But I wouldn't mind the company of your little dog."

"Mr. Brad, I have a confession to make." She looked at him sheepishly when she admitted, "I don't have a dog."

"But what about all the tennis balls I keep having to return to you?"

She shrugged.

Brad shook his head. "You are a crafty one, Miss Em."

"How else could an old lady like me get a handsome man like you to talk to me?"

"A simple hi would have sufficed."

"But it wouldn't be nearly as much fun."

"True… You can keep tossing those balls over if you like."

"Will do, Mr. Brad. Now let me go make you those brownies to cheer you up."

He started back up on the yard, but he'd been doing a good job keeping up with it so there was little for him to do.

Brad settled himself down on the folding chair and looked up at the heavens, feeling utterly bereft. It was a powerless feeling—not knowing if Thane would survive, and having no way to help him.

The thought of losing his best friend was unfathomable.

Poor Brie…

If he was feeling this way, what the hell was she going through?

The young woman held a special place in his heart. She'd won Brad over with her devotion to Thane and her powerful and natural submissive nature. The girl was a ray of light in a sometimes dark world.

She was suffering. Maybe together they could survive the uncertain days ahead.

Guidance

Brad had gone to the hospital several times, but Brie refused to leave Thane's side. Because his friend was in the ICU, no one but close family was permitted to visit. After several failed attempts to see her, he'd stopped trying.

He threw himself into his work with no other avenue for escape. If he couldn't help Thane or Brie, he would give all he had for his students and make these uncertain times counted for something.

Brad had his eyes set on Ms. Slater. She needed to know the satisfaction of fully submitting in humbleness and with true gratitude. A half-hearted gift of submission meant nothing, and was an insult to the Dom mastering the sub.

"For tonight's second practicum, you will be serving several Dominants," he informed the girl.

Baron joined Brad on the stage as Ms. Slater slowly walked up the steps. It was easy to see she was excited by the prospect. "Are we going to be doing DP?" she asked breathlessly.

"We will be taking you through the paces, pleasuring ourselves with the commands we give you. Are you willing to serve us?"

"Oh yes!" she said excitedly. Then, remembering herself, she answered properly, "If it pleases you."

"It does." Brad motioned to the man standing at the entrance of the auditorium. "Sir Reed. Please join us."

Brad watched the expression on the girl's face change as the Dom she had coupled with on the first day walked down the aisle towards them. She did not attempt to hide her disappointment.

As soon as Reed joined them, Brad called her on it. "Ms. Slater, apologize now for disrespecting Sir Reed."

"But I—"

"Now," he commanded harshly.

Ms. Slater turned to him, her eyes downcast. "I am sorry for not..." She stopped, obviously unsure how to word her apology without sounding insulting.

"Spit it out, Ms. Slater. Be honest with the Dom standing in front of you," he demanded.

"Sir Reed, I am sorry for my sour attitude when I heard you were being included in the scene."

The man grabbed her chin and forced her to look him in the eye. "I did not deserve such a welcome, did I?"

"No, Sir Reed, you did not."

"You must be punished for showing such blatant disrespect."

She stared into his eyes, sighing nervously. "Yes, Sir Reed."

Brad was heartened to hear her agreement. At least

the girl understood her mistake needed correction.

"Turn so your back is facing the other students."

She did so slowly, obviously scared but still willing.

"Bend down and grab your ankles," Sir Reed ordered.

Ms. Slater closed her eyes as she assumed the humiliating position. Lifting her skirt, Sir Reed pulled down her panties to her thighs. "Why are you being punished?"

"I was disrespectful to you."

"Had I done anything to you that would justify such treatment?"

"No, Sir Reed."

"Do not make a sound as I spank you."

The smack of palm against flesh echoed through the auditorium. Ms. Slater let out a muffled grunt at the force of the smack.

"I will give you that one, but now that you know how hard it will be, I expect no other sound from you."

She nodded her head between her legs.

Sir Reed gave her nine more powerful smacks that left her ass bright red. He pulled her panties up and laid the material of her skirt back down before ordering her to stand up and face him.

Ms. Slater turned around, silent tears wetting her cheeks. "Have you learned your lesson, Ms. Slater?"

"I have, Sir Reed."

Brad addressed her. "Because of your actions, your scene is done. You may go back and sit down, Ms. Slater. Hopefully, you won't make that mistake again."

She bowed her head. "Yes, Master Anderson."

As she was heading back to her seat, she stopped and

turned around. "I am truly sorry, Sir Reed."

"No need to apologize further, Ms. Slater. You took your punishment, and I hold nothing against you because of it. We begin on a fresh note, as if it never happened," he assured her.

She bowed low to him. "Thank you, Sir Reed."

Brad smiled to himself. He'd known she had potential. Now that her ego had been properly checked, he hoped they would see real growth from her.

He shook Sir Reed's hand, grateful the Dom had been able to get his point across while getting the apology he was due. Both Baron and Sir Reed left the stage together.

Now it was on to his next difficult student…

"Ms. Grady."

The stoic woman got up from her seat and walked up the steps, her face as unreadable as the first night he'd met her.

"The panel and I are concerned by your lack of expression, both physically and verbally."

She just stared at him.

"Can you tell me why that would be a concern for us?"

She looked out over the stage at her classmates. It took her several moments before replying, "I'm not like everyone here, Master Anderson."

"That is not what I asked."

"Master Anderson, I'm a complicated person."

"That answer does not address the question. Are you trying to test me?"

"No, Master Anderson."

"Answer the question in your next breath or you will be dismissed."

There were gasps from the other students. Apparently, they had chosen not to believe his warning that they would dismiss a student if it was deemed necessary. The fact that all the trainers were concerned about her lack of communication skills left him without reservation should he decide it was time for her to leave.

"My silence is disconcerting, Master Anderson."

"It's far more than that. If you were a Dom and you were scening with someone like you, what issue would you face?"

She stared at the other students. He wasn't sure if she was suffering from a feeling of superiority or fear.

"I would not want to scene with someone like me, Master Anderson. If the submissive can't tap into her own feelings, how can the Dominant possibly know where her triggers are?"

"Correct."

She looked to the ground. "Master Anderson, I was hoping you and the trainers here could help me connect with myself. I feel numb inside...dead really."

"That is not the purpose of this course," Brad told her gently, encouraged that she was being honest.

She braved a look at him. "I'm begging you. Don't make me leave." Her gaze returned to the floor.

Brad looked to the panel. Marquis nodded slightly, and Baron gave a smile of approval while Mistress Lou looked undecided.

"Fine, I will scene with you while the rest of the trainers watch. The panel will decide your future depending on how well you do under my command."

She looked defeated, but answered, "As you wish, Master Anderson."

"A proper answer would be, 'Thank you for the second chance.'"

She nodded, amending, "Thank you for the second chance. I will not fail you."

He put his hand on her shoulder. "Now that's more like it."

Brad motioned to an assistant, who brought up a spanking bench and placed it in the middle of the stage.

"You will undress completely, Ms. Grady."

She showed no emotion as she undressed, so he asked, "What are you thinking right now?"

"Nothing. I'm undressing."

"You're not wondering what my plans are for the bench?"

She shrugged, "Yes, I suppose I am."

"Then connect with that curiosity and let it show on your face."

She looked at him, frowning. "How?"

He turned to the other students. "How do you express your curiosity nonverbally?"

Miss Henderson's hand shot up first.

"Yes, Miss Henderson?"

"I glance in the direction of the instrument multiple times, Master Anderson. I can't help myself."

Brad nodded. "Anyone else?"

Miss Rodriguez rose her hand next. "I tend to lick my lips. I guess in expectation of the unknown…"

"Yes, that is a common reaction."

Brad turned back to Ms. Grady. "I want you to be conscious of your thoughts and allow what you are thinking to show on your face and in your action as you finish undressing."

She took a deep breath before proceeding. Her forced glances at the bench were comical, as was the way she licked her lips as if both actions were unnatural to her. However, she was trying and that counted for something.

"Kneel before me, Ms. Grady."

She got down on her knees, and kept her gaze forward with a blank stare.

"Look up at me."

Her gaze moved upwards to meet his.

"You are not limited to actions. Sounds, not words, are also helpful. I want you to make noises that express your thoughts as you unzip my pants and free my cock to suck it."

Her gaze remained glued to his eyes as she fumbled with his pants. Once his large cock was bared, she looked down at it and said, "Hmm…"

Brad had to stifle a laugh. "Ms. Grady, while I appreciate your honest expression, keep your partner in mind. What other way could you express yourself without sounding like you are contemplating an inanimate object."

She actually cracked the tiniest of smiles. "I'm sorry, Master Anderson." She grasped his cock and made a soft moan before opening her lips and encasing the head of his cock in her mouth.

Leading by example, Brad groaned loudly, expressing

his appreciation of her lips. She began sucking with more enthusiasm. "Do you see how my reaction spurred your own?"

She broke off the suction to answer him, and he fisted her hair pushing her mouth back onto his cock. "I did not say to stop. You must answer with my cock in your mouth."

She looked up at him, and let out a long, muffled, "Mmmm…"

Brad smiled down at her. "That's acceptable, Ms. Grady. You may disengage."

She released his cock, her lips making a popping sound as she did so. She sat back down on her heels, her face suddenly becoming blank again as if a light bulb had been switched off.

"Mount the bench," he ordered.

Brad rolled up his sleeves as she climbed onto the bench. He walked up to her slowly and ran his hand over the smooth curve of her buttocks. "Thoughts as I touch you?"

"I don't like it."

"Why?"

Ms. Grady thought for several moments. "It's too soft."

"Ah…" Brad snapped his fingers and the assistant brought a table with several instruments on it.

Brad picked up the crop and showed it to her. "Show me your thoughts about this instrument without words."

The girl stared at it dismissively.

"Based on that response, I would assume you do not care for the instrument or at the very least, have no interested in scening with it."

"True."

"But I think your disinterest is misplaced."

She gave him the briefest look of defiance before returning to her indifferent look.

Brad moved to her side and commanded, "Turn your head toward me. I want to see your reaction as I use it on you."

Ms. Grady stared at him, giving him nothing in her expression.

"Remember, I am *expecting* a reaction."

She nodded, and made a strange face trying to give him something. It was as if the girl was totally disconnected from herself—a third person in the mix—and was faking a reaction for him.

"Don't force it, Ms. Grady, but be conscious of your feelings and thoughts. Let *those* show in your face."

Brad had never experienced anyone like her before. He slapped the crop against her fleshy ass, warming it up.

Her face remained expressionless, but he felt her desperation. She wanted to feel something.

Brad would make sure she did.

Without warning, he slapped her left buttock with authority. She cried out, her eyes registering surprise and then amusement. She looked at Brad, daring him to do it again.

He did, with even greater force.

Ms. Grady gasped, her eyes twinkling—for the first time registering pleasure.

Having a better idea of her pain tolerance, Brad began delivering a volley of alternating strokes. Her ass became red as welts appeared. When she eventually closed her eyes, he stopped.

"Thoughts?"

"I…like it."

"Now I'm going to fuck that smarting ass of yours," he informed her.

Brad set down the crop and positioned himself behind her, spreading her ass cheeks with his hands. He could see she was wet from the crop.

"Continue to look at me, Ms. Grady."

She opened her eyes and stared at him.

Brad dived right in, curious how she would react to his challenging girth. Unlike most women, she did not grimace or show discomfort. On the other hand, she didn't show pleasure either. He might as well be fucking a blow-up doll for all the expression in her face.

Brad pushed in further and finally heard her begin to pant, a common reaction for many women. Needing more, however, he commanded, "Show without words what you are feeling right now."

She had to think about it before she bit her lip.

At least it was something…

"Now, show me with your eyes what you are feeling as I fuck you."

She narrowed her eyes ominously.

What the hell did that mean? "Ms. Grady, what are you trying to express to me?"

"Concentration."

"It looks more like a glare."

Her eyebrows raised in surprise. "Really?"

This woman was a piece of work.

Brad gave her a few more solid strokes before pulling out and ordering her to kneel before him.

"Open your mouth."

She did so as she looked up at him. Yet again, he was facing a vacant expression.

Brad closed his eyes as he stroked his cock, building up his orgasm. He stared down at her as his come shot forth, covering her lips and chest with his manly essence.

She blinked a few times, but that was it.

"Thoughts?" he asked as his come dripped from her chin.

The girl shrugged.

"I need more than that."

"It was like kissing. I'm willing, but it doesn't do anything for me."

He snapped his fingers and the assistant threw him two towels. He handed one to Ms. Grady as he cleaned himself off.

Brad made her face the panel for questioning.

Marquis was the first to speak up. "Ms. Grady, on a scale of one to ten, what would you give the scene?"

She gave Brad a sideways glance before answering, "A four."

"And the reason for that score?" he pressed.

"I like the crop. I didn't know that until now."

Mistress Lou followed her answer with, "Would you say that you are more responsive to pain?"

Ms. Grady shrugged. "Maybe…I guess."

Baron asked her, "What did you learn from the session?"

"That I *am* capable of feeling something."

"That is all for now, Ms. Grady," Brad told her. "The panel and I will discuss your performance and let you know tomorrow if you will be continuing."

"May I speak, Master Anderson?"

"Of course."

She looked at the trainers. "Tonight was probably the best sex I've ever had."

Brad was shocked by her statement and felt sorry for the girl. She was not on the same level as the other students—not by a long shot. If the trainers were to keep her, she would need extra instruction just to keep up.

He wasn't sure if the other trainers would be willing to put in the time, but he would plead his case for her.

Brad sat in his office later that night, having gone through half a box of thin mints as he typed up his thoughts about the night.

He was surprised to hear a knock at the door.

Brad quickly boxed up the remaining cookies and threw them in the drawer, before standing up behind his desk and commanding formally, "Come in."

Marquis Gray entered his office. "May I have a word with you, Headmaster?"

"Certainly," he answered, gesturing to a seat.

"I'd like to offer my time for the student, Ms. Grady."

Brad grinned. "You have hope for her too?"

"I believe she may have masochistic tendencies and not know it. I think I can help her, and am willing to put in needed time."

"I agree with your assessment and will take you up on the offer."

Marquis frowned for a moment and then cleared his throat. "You have something... here," he said, wiping the right side of his own mouth.

Brad licked his lips and tasted the chocolate and crumbs. He chuckled self-consciously. "I was indulging in a guilty pleasure." He pulled out a fresh box and pushed it toward the man. "Please, have some."

"I was wondering why it smelled like a mint factory in here."

"That strong, huh?"

"Out of curiosity, how many have you eaten?"

"A few."

"Stress eating—you?"

Brad sat back in his chair. "I'm concerned about young Brie, but her phone doesn't seem to work when she's at the hospital—I can't even leave a message. I'm feeling very protective toward the girl right now, but she refuses to leave Thane's side despite my numerous visits to the ICU. I have *yet* to see her since the crash."

"I think enough time has passed to throw courtesy out the window."

"Meaning?"

"Demand to see her. Don't take no as an answer."

Brad nodded. He looked down at his snack drawer and smiled. "It sure in the hell beats using up my year's supply of thin mints."

Marquis Gray chuckled as he stood up. "So we're agreed on Ms. Grady?"

"Absolutely."

As he was walking out the door, Brad called out after Marquis, tossing him a box. "Don't forget your thin mints. They'll see you through the darkest of days."

Marquis caught it in one hand, and nodded his thanks before closing the door.

Brad sat back down and pulled out the roll of unopened cookies from the box. He tore the cellophane and began munching again.

Ready or not, young Brie, I'm coming for a visit.

The Damsel

Brad asked to speak to the head nurse. He stuck out his hand to shake hers when she arrived, giving the woman a charming smile to put her at ease. "Hello, I'm Brad Anderson, a good friend to both Mr. and Mrs. Davis. I was wondering if you could let Mrs. Davis know I need to speak with her."

The nurse shook her head. "I'm sorry. Mrs. Davis won't come out to see anyone. She rarely leaves her husband's side, even for herself."

Brad was ready for that and stated, "Do you mind telling her that I *insist* on seeing her? I'm not asking." To emphasize his point, Brad stood with his muscular arms crossed, his feet planted firmly on the ground. "I will not leave until I see her."

The nurse chuckled. "I can certainly relay the message, but I can't guarantee the results."

Brad winked at her. "Something tells me you have the power of persuasion," he leaned closer to look at her tag, "Nurse Abby."

She laughed pleasantly. "I will stress to Mrs. Davis

how serious you are," she assured him as she disappeared between the double doors of the ICU.

Brad was not prepared when Brie finally made her appearance. She looked like the undead with those dark circles under her eyes and the unusual paleness of her skin. He couldn't help but frown when he first saw her.

Brie seemed unnerved by his response and blurted, "Sir's doing better. His color is good, and the physical therapist is working hard on building his muscles so it won't be as difficult to move when he wakes."

"Brie…"

"What is it, Master Anderson?"

"You look terrible. Have you been eating?"

The girl gave him a flurry of excuses, but it was obvious to him that she was nutritionally deprived. Knowing that she was pregnant was concerning—especially because it was Thane's child.

Brad was certain that if his best friend awoke now, he would not be happy to find Brie in such a state. In all honesty, Brad felt responsible seeing her this way. With Thane out for the count, it was his duty to take charge of the situation.

Brie kept insisting she was fine, which irritated him to no end when he could see clearly she was not so he warned her, "I will bend you over and spank you if you say that again," he warned her.

Despite her continued protests, he was able to get Brie to sit while he scrounged up a bowl of soup and the last remaining piece of fresh fruit from the cafeteria.

Although it wasn't much, at least it was something.

He continued to grill her as she ate, and was actually

inspired by her feisty attitude when she answered him. The young woman was a spitfire, no doubt about it, but she needed some reining in.

When Brie confessed that Thane seemed just like his mother, the thought of it gave him icy chills. Brad instinctively grabbed her in a bear hug and held her tight. It was a shock to him when a few moments later she suddenly broke down and started to cry.

It was as if he had released a dam inside her. Once the girl began, there was no stopping the flood of emotion. All Brad could do was hold on tight and let the tidal wave pour out from her. He ignored the passersby who stared at them, wanting only to protect the hurting girl.

When the torrent finally stopped, both of them were a mess. He laughed when she patted his sopping wet shirt and apologized. Ripping the soaked material from his body, he got up and grabbed her a box of Kleenex.

"Tears dry up, but bottled emotions fester. Now blow," he commanded gently. Brad looked down at her with a feeling of such deep tenderness it almost crushed his heart. She'd been through so much on her own...

After he had her cleaned up and presentable, he took the numerous tissues and tossed them away, garnering the attention of a nurse passing by. Well, it couldn't be helped. His chest had that kind of effect on women.

Brad chuckled as he explained the reason for his state of undress. "My shirt was sacrificed for the damsel in distress," he told her, pointing to Brie.

When the nurse offered to personally dry it for him, he immediately agreed and gave her a tip of an imaginary hat and an extra flex of his chest muscles as payment.

He looked back at Brie when the nurse left, finally understanding his role in all this.

"Brie, I'm going to be watching over you until Thane wakes."

She immediately dismissed his offer. "I can't drive all the way from your home to the hospital every day. It's too far."

He smiled amiably. "I know this, young Brie. That's why I'll be staying with you—along with Cayenne, of course."

Her eyes lit up at the mention of the orange tabby.

"See? I already have you smiling." It did his heart a world of good to see that smile. He couldn't explain why.

When it looked as if she was about to refuse his offer, Brad informed her, "You do not have a say in this. I refuse to suffer the wrath of Thane to placate your ego."

She swayed on her feet, giving him the final ammo needed to get her to submit to his will. "You're only helping my case. Now you go back to your husband and explain to him that you will be back bright and early tomorrow."

He could tell how reluctant she was to leave Thane's side. The girl would do anything for the man—even sacrifice herself. Such devotion should be rewarded, not punished by fate and the powers above.

He watched her leave to say good-bye, and then growled under his breath as he looked up toward the heavens. "You better do right by her!"

Brad was horrified when they made it to Thane's apartment and he started browsing through the pantry. It was filled with old folk's nutritional drinks and soda crackers. No wonder the girl was so sickly...

After scolding her, he formally apologized to the child by getting down on his knees and speaking to her stomach. "Hey baby bump, I'm sorry. I had no idea your mommy was abusing you."

It made Brie smile—a small victory.

He then informed her that he was leaving to get groceries and pick up Cayenne.

The sparkle in her eye at the mention of the kitten pleased him. He was sure with proper food and a little feline loving, Brie would be okay.

"It *will* be nice to have some life in this place," she admitted to him, but then her smile faded and he saw the tears well up. "God, I miss him."

Brad felt a stab to his chest, missing Thane's presence as well. All he could do to survive it was to wrap her in a tight embrace, but he couldn't handle her crying again. Her pain brought out a side of him he wasn't willing to release. He instinctually knew that the need to protect her could easily grow into something much deeper, so he warned Brie, "I'm no good with tears."

Out of self-defense, he started to tickle her.

Brie burst out in giggles as she squirmed in his arms. "Go get that kitten already, and leave me be," she scolded when he let her go. Before he left, she asked,

"Master Anderson, do you mind if I sleep with Cayenne tonight?"

Grateful for her change of mood, he answered somberly, "Not at all. I'm sure she would prefurrrr that."

The expression on her face was comical and reminded him why humor was always the best place to go whenever he was in doubt.

Brad left Brie to run his errands, feeling better about the entire situation. As long as he kept his mind clear and his humor ready, he could be what she needed.

Thane would expect no less from him.

Upon his return, he was heartened to see the connection between Brie and Cayenne when the two were reunited. The girl was smiling again…

"While you ladies get reacquainted, I'll make my famous tomato bisque for tomorrow, so it can start simmering. I'm determined to make that baby bump happy."

He set to work, pouring his soul into his cooking. It was the one thing he could do for Brie that no one else could. He firmly believed there was a transfer of power in cooking. From the life of the fresh vegetables, the respect of the ingredients, to the care and love infused into even the simplest dish, positive energy was released into the recipient whenever it was consumed.

"She's just too darn cute," Brie declared from the couch.

He chuckled as he finished cooking two grilled cheese, turning over the perfectly golden-brown sandwiches. "Yes, she's the best companion a man could ask for."

"Except for a devoted submissive, of course," Brie protested.

"Trust me, Cayenne is *far* less complicated." He thought of his conflicted feelings about Shey and laughed again.

Brie tsked. "But I didn't get you Cayenne so you could continue living a solitary life."

Brad walked over to her with two lovingly crafted grilled cheese—his personal comfort food of choice. He nearly tripped over Cayenne when the cat rubbed up against his leg. Luckily, he was used to the feline's adoration and avoided injury to both himself and her.

Shrugging as he handed over Brie's plate, he said, "You know, there's nothing wrong with being alone, Mrs. Davis."

Brie looked up at him with a frown. "No, there isn't, unless you have a soulmate waiting for you somewhere."

Brad felt another stab to his heart thinking of Shey. He cleared his throat, her assertion making him more than just a little uncomfortable. "Hmm…"

He sat down beside her and heard a long, muffled farting sound escape from under his sofa cushion.

"Really, Master Anderson, I'm trying to eat." The little minx giggled.

Brad threw his head back and laughed so hard, tears came to his eyes. "Oh hell…I needed that."

Leave it to Brie, a woman suffering in her own pain, to make *him* laugh with a well-placed whoopee cushion. He determined right then that he would never abandon her, no matter how tough the road ahead.

The two would walk that fine line of friendship, and

use jesting and pranks as their safety valve. It could work.

He smiled at Brie's purr of pleasure after she took a bite of his sandwich. "Nothing like a grilled cheese sandwich."

"Melty goodness for the soul," he agreed, taking his own bite before breaking off a piece for Cayenne. The little lioness licked his offering several times before gracefully taking it from his hand.

Always the gracious lady, he thought, proud of his kitten.

"I can't wait to meet you here for dinner tomorrow, Master Anderson. It's been a while since I had anyone waiting for me at home," Brie confessed.

Brad put his arm around her protectively. "All that's changed now." He looked down at her and added reproachfully, "You know that you only needed to reach out, and I would have been by your side in a heartbeat."

She shrugged her delicate shoulders. "My sole focus this whole time—the only thing I care about—is seeing Sir open his eyes. Even now, I'm panicking inside because he might wake up and I won't be there."

Brad shook his head. "Thane doesn't need you to live at the hospital 24/7, young Brie."

Her honey-colored eyes bore into his soul when she answered, "It's not what he needs, it's about what I need. I have to be there when Sir awakens."

His heart rate increased, her deep-seated determination stirring something in him. In an effort to keep things light, he stated, "And you will be—looking all rosy-cheeked and giddy, the picture of health. Then he will turn to me and say, 'Well done, Brad. Way to take care of my girl while I was out for the count.'"

"That will not be the first thing out of his mouth," she insisted.

He held out his hand to shake hers. "Wanna bet?"

She replied confidently, "Ten bucks."

"Fine, show me yours and I will show you mine."

He watched Brie grab a ten-dollar bill out of her purse and place it on the coffee table. He whipped out his wallet and put down a twenty, snagging her ten.

"Ha, I was needing a ten."

He took the twenty and walked over, placing it on Thane's work desk. "When it comes time to collect on the bet, we can explain it to him."

She snorted in pleasure. "Good, because I've already decided what to buy with it."

"What?"

Brie grinned evilly to herself, making him curious what she had in mind, but the minx only answered, "My secret."

Brad chuckled. The girl truly was a spitfire. He looked forward to the day he lost the bet and found out exactly what she was smiling about.

Through effort, determination, and thoughtful care, he was certain he could help make young Brie whole again.

He found she was still up when he returned late from

The Center, busily scribbling away in a journal. "Keeping a record of your thoughts?" he asked, surprised that she was still up.

She blushed when she answered. "Not exactly." She held up the journal, showing him the cover. "Does this look familiar to you?"

He smirked. "That wouldn't be your fantasy journal, would it?"

"It is, indeed. It makes me feel closer to Sir whenever I write in it. I figure if it worked bringing us together when we were apart traveling, why not do it now for the same purpose? Plus, it will give Sir some entertaining reading when he wakes."

Brad smiled, nodding. "Seems like a worthy endeavor on many counts."

Her eyes twinkled. "You want to read the latest entry? I'm curious if you've ever come across a girl with a similar fantasy as a trainer." She grinned down at the journal as she handed it to him, blushing again.

"Well, you've got my curiosity piqued, but are you certain you want me to read it?"

"Yes, and be honest afterward."

"Honest about what?"

Brie giggled. "If you've ever come across something like it as a trainer."

"Sure." Brad took the journal from her, wondering where her mind was at.

I am so excited! I'm on my first international trip and it is on the beautiful beaches of Rio de Janeiro. My parents are so overly protective that I have never been outside the United States before.

They watch me like a hawk, especially now that I am getting older and my curves are starting to fill out.

Hell, my curfew is ten PM, for Christ's sake. How lame is that? It makes me the butt of jokes from my friends. But I tell ya, no one was laughing when I told them where I was headed for my Christmas vacation.

Rio is well-known for sexy people and topless beaches.

I'm going to be exposed to it all in one fell swoop. Under the watchful eyes of my parents—of course.

I told you how protective they are, right...

* * *

I'm tanning beside the pool, with the ocean just beyond. It seems silly to me that my parents would rather swim in a pool than dip their feet in the actual ocean just a few hundred yards away. But, hey, they get a full-service bar at the pool and can still keep an eye on me.

My mom is busy reading some stupid mystery novel, and my dad is talking to an old British dude with a huge gut. I've chosen to get as far away from them as they will allow, and am lying peacefully in the beautiful Rio sun, taking in its life-giving rays.

"American?" a deep voice asks.

I open my eyes to an Adonis of a man. A beautiful creature of bronze skin, chiseled features, and dark brown eyes that ensnare me.

"Yes," I answer meekly, sitting up a little straighter as he smiles down at me.

"You are the most beautiful woman I have ever seen."

I blush a deep red and giggle, only helping to highlight my lack of experience with this kind of exchange.

"And your laughter, it is quite charming."

His comment only makes me giggle more, furthering my embarrassment.

"Have you been to Rio before?"

I smile shyly as I answer, my whole being mesmerized by this man. "No, this is my first time."

"Are you alone?"

I sigh, not thrilled to admit the truth but too new at this to do anything else. "No, my parents are over there," I tell him, pointing to the two.

"Ah…they seem nice."

I snort. "They're very protective."

He looks at me with magnetic eyes and I stare up at him unabashedly. I can't help it.

The man is perfection….

He raises an eyebrow, making me swoon inside.

"How old are you?"

From out of nowhere, I answer coyly, "Old enough."

He takes my assertion as fact and asks, "Would you join me on the beach?"

I glance at my parents.

"See that towel over there? It's in plain sight of your mother and father."

I put my hand to my forehead to shield my eyes and look where he is pointing. Sure enough, there is a large, colorful towel lying in the sand.

"You will be safe," he says, holding his hand out to me.

I know I should tell my parents, but this man is too gorgeous and the towel is not far enough away to be concerned. Besides, there are tons of beachgoers walking about.

I take his hand and he pulls me up to him. Oh my God, he's so tall and his torso so ripped. I think I have just died and gone to heaven.

The Adonis picks up my skirt cover-up and instructs me to slip it on. I am touched by his gentlemanly ways. He leads me straight to the towel, and I feel my defenses start to ease. He gestures that I lie down first and then he joins me. I lay there, not believing my luck. I have waited all my life for a moment like this. The man is pure sexual energy.

He props his head against his hand and stares down at me as if I truly am the most beautiful thing he has seen. I can't help but blush.

"Do you mind if I kiss you?"

I instinctually glance in the direction of my parents and see that neither has noticed I've moved—both thoroughly focused on their own activities.

My Adonis follows my gaze and smiles down at me. "Well?"

I just smiled nervously and nod.

Holding my breath, I watch his gorgeous lips descend on me, and moan lightly when I feel their firm touch for the first time.

Holy hell…

His kiss begins gently, drawing me in with his natural masculine dominance. Soon, however, I feel the pressure of his tongue as it demands access. I open my lips and groan loudly when his tongue thrusts in and he tastes me.

Oh God, I never knew what I was missing…

My body is humming with desire as this man takes over my soul with his possessive kisses. I come up for air every time he stops, only to drown in him again when he claims my mouth.

That's when I feel the tentative touch of his fingers along the material of my bikini as he grazes my breast. I stiffen in his arms, having never been touched in that way, but I do not resist. I give in to the feelings he is inciting from deep in my feminine soul. I don't want him to stop.

He breaks the kiss again and murmurs in a low voice, "Your breasts are so perfect. They beg for my attention."

I look around, certain people must be staring, but no one seems to care and my parents continue reading and talking.

"Touch me," I beg.

He smiles hungrily as he kisses me again, driving out any reservations as his hands glide over my bathing suit, teasing my nipples. They are hard and aching, as is the area between my legs. I never knew a man could make me feel like this.

"Have you ever made love to a man?" he asks.

My eyes pop open as my heart begins to beat even faster. "No," I whisper, sounding almost apologetic in my answer, not wanting him to stop.

I see a spark in his eye, as if my answer pleases him. He leans down again and takes my breath away with his deep kiss.

"Would you let me be your first?"

I stop breathing altogether as I stare at him.

I feel him gently lift the material of my cover-up skirt as he moves me onto my side so he can spoon against me, pressing the bulge in his swimming trunks against my ass.

I am now facing my parents, in the middle of a crowded beach, with a man who wants to make love to me.

He turns my head toward him and kisses me again, stealing all reason as his hands glide over my body, lingering on my nipples, creating an even greater ache for him.

This time when Adonis pulls away, he asks, "May I?"

"I..."

"I want to connect with you," he murmurs in a husky voice. "No one will know if you keep silent. It will only look to others *that we are cuddling." He kisses me again, pressing his hardness against me. "Only you and I will know the truth that my manhood is deep inside you."*

I do not know why his last words stir me, but I know with certainty that I will regret saying no and never knowing such a connection with him. Still…we are in public and I am afraid.

He can read the fear in my eyes, and smiles confidently. "No one will know, my beauty. Let me connect with you."

My breath comes in short gasps as I nod my consent.

I lay my head on the towel, directly facing my parents. I can feel him fiddling with the material of my bathing suit under my cover-up, his movements slow so as to attract no attention. He pulls my bottoms down so that my ass is now bare under the material of the cover-up.

He then cuddles against me, one arm wrapped around my torso while the other one that is unseen frees his manhood from his suit and I feel the hardness of a man's shaft press against my sex for the first time.

I glance down, feeling exposed, but am shocked to see how innocent we look. The material of my cover-up hides from prying eyes the naughtiness of what we are about to do.

I lay my head back down, feeling more confident and eager for whatever he plans to do.

My Adonis doesn't thrust his shaft, but leans down and starts kissing my neck. People walk around us, seeing only a couple who appear to be in love embracing each other intimately. They don't give us a second glance.

I stare across the sand at my parents, in shock that this moment is about to happen right under their noses. Their precious daughter is about to lose her virginity to this beautiful Adonis in broad daylight.

"*Whatever you do, don't make a sound,*" *he cautions as he lowers his arm to rest against my pelvis as his shaft presses harder against my virgin hole. I gasp as the discomfort starts, but he murmurs softly,* "*Shhh…*"

Tears well up in my eyes as the pain of his entry takes over. I want to scream, but I am silent as a single tear forms and falls from my eye.

Suddenly, his large manhood breaks through my virginal resistance and pushes deep inside me.

My whole body becomes numb as chills take over in response to this foreign invasion.

I look over at my parents as the single tear continues to fall slowly down my cheek.

The Adonis turns my head toward him again, kissing me with passion he'd held back until now. His movements are so slight that no one would notice, but I am consumed by his slow thrusts as he moves deeper and deeper inside my body.

When his hands begin caressing my hard nipples, I feel the deep ache again, the one that invited this invasion, and I am satisfied. I need his hardness to fill me up.

I close my eyes as people walk by us, ignoring them as I concentrate on the pressure and movement of his shaft.

"*I am making love to you,*" *he growls in my ear.*

My pussy contracts around him, accepting his truth.

"*Kiss me,*" *he demands.*

I turn my head and offer my lips to him. As he leans in for the kiss, he pushes even farther inside my sex. I can't breathe.

The man consumes me with his body and mouth.

When he breaks away and I look back to my parents, I see that both are now looking around wildly. They have finally noticed I am missing.

I tense, feeling the overwhelming instinct to flee, but Adonis stares at them as he holds me tight. "I am going to come inside you now."

His cock stills and I start to feel the pulsing of his shaft as his warm seed fills my soul to bursting. My father spots us from across the pool and calls out to my mother as they start toward us.

Adonis gives me one last thrust as he kisses me on the cheek. He slowly disengages and covers up my ass with my bikini bottom, carefully straightening the material of my cover-up afterward.

He pretends not to see my father rushing toward us as he adjusts himself with his unseen hand while tilting my head up with a finger of the other. He kisses me gently in front of my parents.

"What the hell is going on there!" my father bellows.

Adonis smiles cordially as he stands up, holding out his right hand to my father. "I asked your beautiful daughter to join me on my towel, sir."

My father snarls, looking him up and down disapprovingly. "She is far too young for the likes of you." He grabs my arm, pulling me beside him protectively.

Adonis puts his hand to his chest. "I am sorry if I offended."

"It's not right to drag a girl off without her parents knowing," my mother sputters.

"He didn't drag me off, Mama," I protest, finally finding my voice. "I was right here all the time."

Adonis winks at me, and my heart melts.

"You are too old to be kissing innocent girls," my father roars protectively.

"Again, I am sorry for offending you." Adonis turns to me and takes my hand, kissing it all gentlemanly-like. "It was a pleasure connecting with you."

I don't want him to leave, but know this is good-bye. I will

*never know his kiss again or the feel of his masculinity inside me.
"The pleasure was mine."*

*Adonis picks up his colorful towel to leave, but not before I
notice the bloodstain on it. Physical evidence of my lost virginity.*

My parents don't notice it.

*"You're going back to the hotel room, young lady. Apparently,
I need to lecture you again about not talking to strangers."*

*I would have been dying of embarrassment at the loud scene my
father was causing, but—I'm officially a woman now.*

Both Adonis and I know that.

I gaze at him longingly as my father drags me away.

*Adonis smiles, nodding his head. That beautiful man will
always and forever be my first…*

While he read, Brad nonchalantly put a pillow from
the couch over his lap and called Cayenne to him so he
could pet her. He'd done it as a precaution to hide any
reaction he might have to her unusual fantasy.

The decision was a smart one, as he'd found it quite
arousing.

"Well?" Brie asked when he closed the journal.

He raised his eyebrows. "Have I ever come across a
similar fantasy? No, I can't say I've ever read anything
quite like this."

"It is too disturbing?"

He chuckled. "Disturbing? Not at all."

"I don't know what's wrong with me, but the idea of
a man taking a virgin in public with no one aware—while
she's under her parents' protective watch—totally turns
me on."

Brad smiled. "Do you think your fantasy might be in

reaction to how you were raised? I mean, your father is the overly protective type."

"Please don't tell me that my sexual fantasies have anything to do with my parents," she whimpered.

"Naturally our upbringing can have an influence on our sexual lives. It's nothing to be ashamed of or even concerned about, young Brie. I personally find this fantasy charming because the girl is empowered by the secret, albeit public, deflowering."

Brie breathed a sigh of relief. "Oh good. I was really hoping you would tell me you see this fantasy all the time, but I still like your answer."

He handed the journal back to her. "Your creativity is fascinating. I'm sure your Master enjoys role-playing these with you."

She smiled again, which gratified him.

"We do, Master Anderson. Thank you for your insight."

Brie pressed the journal to her chest and headed off to bed. Brad picked up Cayenne, placing her on the floor, and lifted the pillow. His shaft was still hard after reading her unusual scenario.

"Down boy," he commanded.

Getting up stiffly, he went to the kitchen and starting chopping vegetables for tomorrow's meal.

Aftermath

Brad felt sick when he was informed Brie had fainted and was unconscious at the hospital. The nurse who met him at the door hurriedly explained that Thane's sister, Lilly, had come to visit and they'd allowed her into Thane's room, having no idea there was a restraining order against her.

He looked down at Brie, his heart breaking inside. He shook his fist angrily up at the heavens. "I told you to do right by this girl, damn it!"

Brad called Thane's attorney while he sat waiting for Brie to awaken. He wanted the man's advice on what needed to be done to prevent another unwanted encounter.

Thompson explained, "You need to file a police report and if you see Lilly again, call the police immediately. She is breaking the law by being anywhere near Mrs. Davis."

"Understood."

With that taken care of, all Brad could do was sit and wait, but waiting was not something he did well. He paced around the hospital anxiously, unable to sit still more than a few minutes.

One prevailing thought kept ringing in his head. *I failed to protect her...*

The relief he felt when Brie finally opened her eyes was overpowering. She smiled up at him as she gazed into his eyes, but her pleasant expression soon turned into excruciating pain as her memories came flooding back.

The girl had been completely shaken by the encounter with Thane's half-sister, so he assured her, "I called Thane's attorney about Lilly and he's on it."

Instead of looking relieved, she seemed even more distraught. "Do you know why she came to the hospital?"

"Thane told me about the incident in China. She's obviously come back to stir up trouble while he is lying unconscious in the hospital. A despicable act from a cowardly woman."

"What did Mr. Thompson tell you when you spoke with him?" she asked hesitantly.

"He advised that you make a police report and call them if she should attempt to contact you again. I have already informed everyone at the hospital about the restraining order against her. She won't be getting in here again."

Brie still looked uneasy. "Did you see her, Master Anderson?"

"No," he growled, pissed that anyone would dare to harass Brie at a time like this.

It shocked Brad when Brie insisted on seeing

Thane's lawyer. What the hell had her running so scared? No matter how much he prodded Brie, she wouldn't tell him what had happened with Lilly.

When he still wasn't convinced, Brie struggled to get up from the hospital bed, claiming she would go to the lawyer alone if she had to. At that point, he finally gave in. If the girl felt that unsettled, it was his duty to see her there safely, no matter how angry he was about being kept in the dark.

"Are you going to say good-bye to Thane before we go?" he asked her.

Brie turned away from him when she answered. "No."

It wasn't until her refusal to say good-bye to Thane that Brad understood just how serious things were. He grabbed her shoulders and forced her to face him.

"Holy hell, what has that witch done to you?"

Brie dropped her gaze, unwilling to look him in the eye, and started to cry.

"I will strangle that woman to within an inch of her life when I see her!"

"Don't go anywhere near Lilly, please," she begged, the fear easy to read on her face.

It only served to anger him further. "You *do* realize it's my duty to protect you."

"If you care about Sir, you will heed my warning."

Brad growled in frustration, tired of these games when it was obvious that Lilly posed a real threat.

"Promise me," Brie insisted.

He snarled irritably, distressed by her odd behavior. "This is not like you—this is beneath you."

"Master Anderson, Lilly has the power to change the course of our lives. Any direct contact might set off a chain of events that we won't recover from," she warned ominously.

Brie was clearly terrified of the woman and there was nothing he could do about it other than to get her to the damn lawyer as soon as possible. He sincerely hoped the man could talk some sense into the girl since he could not.

Brad stood idly by while she met with Thompson in private. It was inconceivable that Thane's bitch of a half-sister was terrorizing Brie—especially now. With Thane incapacitated, Brie was far too fragile to handle the insane woman's antics.

When Brie finally emerged from the lawyer's office, she seemed more like herself and he naturally assumed things were okay.

"Will you tell me what's going on now?"

"No, under the advisement of my lawyer."

Brad was stunned and could only shake his head in disbelief. "She's legitimately got you running scared."

"As Sir's friend, I need you not to engage Lilly in any way."

Her request alarmed Brad, knowing it had to have come from the lawyer. "I give you my word, but I'd prefer to know why."

Instead of answering him, Brie wrapped her arms around him, pressing her head against his chest. "I wish I could tell you."

He now understood that whatever Lilly held over Brie was a direct threat to Thane. Brad grasped her shoulders and gazed into her eyes. "Never question Thane's integrity. He is one of the most honorable men I know."

"I agree…"

"And yet you still doubt," he stated in disbelief. Brad was stunned and asked pointedly, "Do you not carry the brand of your Master?"

Brie nodded in answer.

"Did you not vow to love him through better and worse?"

He saw her bottom lip quiver, but she nodded again.

"Whatever has you questioning that must be profound."

"It is."

Her answer hit him in the gut. She distrusted Thane—the man who'd both collared and married her.

That was simply not acceptable.

He insisted she hold on to what she knew was true, but when Brie answered that she would *try*, he declared, "Succeeding is what Thane would expect."

Brad suspected that if Lilly sensed any weakness in Brie, the witch would go for the jugular, possibly causing irreparable damage to both Brie and Thane. So he felt a real sense of relief when Brie asked if she could go back to the hospital to say good-bye to his friend.

He needed these two to remain a strong couple. If Thane and Brie couldn't make it, what in the hell chance did he have? He settled down in the waiting room, grabbing an old magazine and flipped through it mindlessly, wondering what the future held for all of them.

Brad stood up when Brie came running out of the

ICU crying joyously, "Master Anderson, Sir's eyes are open!"

"He's awake?"

"You have to come see, Master Anderson! You have to see," she insisted, pulling him toward the closed doors.

Nurse Abby came out to let Brie know Dr. Hessen had been called. She purposely looked the other way when Brie pulled Brad through the threshold of the ICU.

Following behind Brie, he was excited to spy Thane through the glass, his eyes very much open. As he approached his friend, however, Brad quickly realized that Thane was not conscious.

He lay there motionless, unresponsive to Brie's excited voice as she called out his name.

Abby came into the room to check his vitals. "The doctor will be here soon," she informed Brie. She looked up at Brad, exchanging a glance that confirmed to him that Thane was still in a vegetative state.

In a sense, nothing had changed.

Brie squeezed Brad's hand. "I asked Sir to give me a sign. I begged him to. And then, just before I was about to leave, I looked back and saw his eyes were open."

Brad only nodded, not wanting to crush her new-found hope.

Dr. Hessen entered the room and started assessing Thane's state of consciousness, calling out his name several times, flicking his cheek and holding up his hand and letting it drop.

Brie peppered her with a number of questions, but the doctor remained focused on her task and did not answer them until the testing was complete.

"Mrs. Davis, he is still unconscious," she announced.

Brie let out a stifled cry, not wanting to believe it.

"However, the fact his eyes are open is a good sign."

"Do you think he did this on purpose? To let me know he can hear me?" Brie asked in a pleading tone.

Dr. Hessen gave her a gentle look. "He certainly may have, Mrs. Davis, but I cannot confirm from a medical standpoint. What I do know, however, is that this is one more sign that he is improving."

"How long until he awakens?" Brie asked excitedly.

"No one can predict that. Some patients become conscious after a few hours, others remain this way for months before recovering, and unfortunately around five to ten percent never do." When the doctor saw the devastation on Brie's face she added, "However, I have every reason to believe this is a positive step forward in Mr. Davis's recovery."

Brie looked at Sir, her eyes brimming with tears. "I know you did this, Sir. I know you heard me…"

Brad stared down at Thane, disturbed by how still and unresponsive he was. This was the first time he'd seen his friend since the crash, and it was sobering. Thane was a strong, commanding individual, but seeing him now, so still amongst all those tubes and wires—it made the man look small and vulnerable.

"You've got to pull out of it, Thane," he stated. "Brie needs you, buddy."

Brad hoped to see some flicker of recognition or response, but Thane remained unnaturally still—like the dead.

He shivered at the thought and put his arm around Brie. "It's going to be okay, young Brie. Thane is tough. He ain't giving up."

She nodded, her whole body trembling as she looked up at him with fresh hope in her eyes.

Gazing down at Brie, Brad thought, *Thane may be tough, but you have a will of iron.*

He squeezed her even tighter.

And I'll be damned if I'll let anyone hurt you.

Brad found a delivery waiting for Brie outside the door of the apartment. He picked it up before entering and was pleasantly surprised to see the gift was from Samantha.

He was glad the Domme was reaching out to Brie. If the community knew how much she was suffering, they would have flooded her with support. But Brie didn't want anyone to know, especially now that Lilly was involved. She'd been very adamant about presenting a strong front to everyone—including all her friends.

Although Brad questioned her decision, he respected it, knowing this was her battle to fight. He agreed not to call in reinforcements, but that didn't mean he wouldn't at some point. The girl didn't seem to know her own limits.

To be honest, Brad admired Brie's stubbornness, as well as the deep love she held for Thane. It amazed him, actually, how well Brie had handled the crash and its aftermath. Even when her Master's integrity was called into question, she'd made the choice to stand beside her man and keep fighting—never losing hope. Damn, what Brad wouldn't give to know such love and devotion himself...

"Looks like you got flowers," he announced as he entered her apartment.

"Really?" Brie asked, getting up from her desk. "Who are they from?"

He grinned. "They're from Colorado."

"Oh my goodness, Lea shouldn't have!" Brie cried in delight, hugging the vase and pressing her face into the arrangement of flowers, looking an awful lot like Cayenne with catnip.

"Well, she didn't," he informed her.

Brie crinkled her brow and removed the card attached, reading it out loud. "To Brie: A reminder of the beauty of life in dark times. I'm thinking of you, and sending my prayers for Thane. Call me should you need anything. ~Samantha Clark."

She tilted her head, staring a long time at the note as if she were reading extra meaning into the simple message.

"Well, that was mighty nice of her," he stated, breaking the silence.

Brie looked up at him with an expression he could not interpret. "Yes, it was very kind."

She placed the card on the table and carried the bouquet to her room. Upon her return she said almost apologetically, "I wanted to wake up to something pretty in the morning. That room has been like a tomb since the crash." She leaned down and gave the cat a scratch on the head. "Of course, Cayenne has also helped with that."

"She has that effect on people," he agreed.

Brie's cell rang. He didn't miss the unpleasant look when she saw who was calling.

"It's not Lilly, is it?" he asked in concern.

"No, but it *is* Mr. Thompson." Brie took a deep breath before hitting the answer button.

Brad watched her face carefully, looking for any signs of distress. Instead of looking upset, she looked confused. "What kind of delivery?"

She frowned, forcing Brad to demand, "Is everything okay?"

Brie looked up at him, her eyes filling with tears. Brad instantly thought the worst, but hid it with a forced smile.

She nodded as she continued to listen to the lawyer. "Sure, I'm at the apartment now. Go ahead and send it." She hung up the phone, a tear falling down her cheek. In a hollow voice she told Brad, "Master Gannon is dead."

"Gannon?"

"The head of the Sanctuary in Montana."

"The place the Wolf Pup and Mary went to?"

Brie nodded. "He passed away two nights ago. Apparently, he had an aggressive form of cancer and died before he had a chance to fight it." She slowly sat down on the couch, a far-off look in her eye.

"Pardon me for asking, but what has that got to do with you?"

Her lip trembled. "I was named in his will for some

197

reason." She looked away to hide the tears that had started to fall.

Brad didn't dare go near her. Her distress was calling out to his protective nature, and he was struggling hard to keep it in check.

Instead of physically comforting her and possibly crossing that line of friendship, he went straight into the kitchen to start a pot of French onion soup. There were times humor wasn't called for, but soup could fill the gap.

"I can't handle this…" she whimpered, suddenly behind him. He felt her arms wrap around his waist as she laid her cheek against his broad back.

Brad closed his eyes to keep his mind focused. "You have to be brave, no matter what the future brings."

"I'm tired of being brave."

He turned around slowly, feeling nothing but sympathy for the girl. "We all get to that point, young Brie. That's why we have to call on our friends. Who do you want me to call for you?"

"Nobody." She looked up at him in agony. "Just stop the hurt. Please…"

Her plea hit him directly in the chest and he felt his eyes start to water. Damn… Thinking fast on his feet, he stated soothingly, "That's why I'm making you soup. But the damn onions are doing a number on my eyes. You'd better stand back, young lady."

He turned around and began chopping the onions with unrestrained zeal.

Damn it, Thane. You need to get your ass back here—pronto. The girl can't survive much more of this shit.

Brie drifted through the house like a ghost, with Cayenne trailing after her, while she waited for the mysterious package to arrive.

Brie jumped when she heard the knock on the door. Brad washed off his hands and said, "Let me get that, darlin'."

He opened the door and looked down at the plastic carrier the man held in his hand, a smile creeping across his lips as he invited the courier in.

"Mrs. Brianna Davis?" the man asked when he saw Brie staring out the window.

"Yes," Brie answered meekly, not turning to face him.

The courier held up a clipboard. "I just need you to sign that you received the animal."

Brie whipped around. "Animal?"

A low, tortured howl sounded from within the plastic carrier.

Brie ignored the man, falling to her knees as she unlatched the small door. She peeked inside, her voice breaking when she called out softly, "Shadow."

There was another tortured cry that caused Cayenne to run to Brad for protection, climbing up his arm to settle on his shoulder.

Brie reached in and slowly pulled out a giant black cat.

The courier stared at her in disbelief. "No one has been able to get near that psycho animal."

Brie ignored his comment as she wrapped her arms around Shadow and cradled him to her chest. Her soulful cry echoed the tormented howl of the animal as the two mourned together.

The courier looked at Brad for help, holding out his clipboard and pen.

"Just give them a moment," Brad stated, digging out a twenty from his wallet and handing it to the man.

"Oh Shadow, I'm so sorry," Brie whispered through her tears, stroking the huge beast. "You must miss your Master so…"

The two were lost in shared grief. The sight just about did Brad in, and he had to look away.

Brie finally stood, wiping away the tears. She took the pen the courier offered with one hand while still holding the huge cat. Scribbling her signature, Brie nodded dully to the man and then started walking toward her bedroom.

Brad understood she needed time to process. At least that huge cat and she could do it together. He patted Cayenne on the head before ushering the courier out the door.

Brad went back to his onions. If he shed an actual tear or two during the process, what did it matter?

Boa Meets the Whip

While they were eating a quick breakfast of leftover steak and eggs, Brad casually mentioned, "I've been asked by Mistress Lou to do a scene with Boa."

Brie stopped mid-bite and stared at him. "Boa and you..."

He nodded.

Brie bit her lip, a dreamy look coming over her face. "That is not something I ever imagined you doing, but it'd be really sexy to watch."

"It is a special favor for the Mistress because Boa expressed an interest."

"When is it happening?"

"Sunday night at The Haven. It's less busy and won't interfere with our work schedules at the Training Center."

"Wow..."

"I was wondering, Brie, since this will probably be the one and only time I do it, would you like to film the scene?"

She sighed and took another bite of her eggs. "I

don't know, Master Anderson. I don't think I should leave Sir's side just to film a scene."

"It's only one night, and you can return to the hospital as soon as we're done."

Brie sighed more heavily. "It's not just Sir I'm worried about. Honestly, I don't know if I could handle being around a bunch of people right now."

Brad knew she needed to get out among the living again, but he was also familiar with her stubborn ways. Rather than push the issue, he said simply, "Well, give it some thought. Personally, I'd like it to be recorded for posterity's sake." He winked at her as he took a bite and slowly chewed.

Brie picked up the last piece of steak from her plate and fed it to Shadow. Ever since the enormous black cat had made his appearance, Brad had noticed a strange connection between the two. Sometimes Brie would talk to the cat as if he were a person, and darn if that cat wouldn't nod or narrow his eyes as if he understood exactly what Brie had said.

It was uncanny.

In response to Brie's generosity toward the beast, and not wanting Cayenne to feel left out, Brad fed the orange tabby a piece of steak as well. He patted the top of her head as she demurely munched the morsel. "Now you stay far away from that Shadow character. Last thing I need is you hanging around the likes of him."

Shadow stared hard at Brad as if he was either offended or silently agreed with Brad's assessment—the man couldn't tell which.

He whispered to his little tabby, "Stay *far, far*

away…"

Sunday morning Brie knocked on Brad's door.

"Come in," he called out.

She stepped inside, but when she saw he was in bed she suddenly became shy and gazed down at the floor. "I've given it a lot of thought, Master Anderson. I agree it'd be a shame not to record your scene with Boa. I am going to put my camera equipment in my car before I leave and will drive down to The Haven to meet you before it starts."

He smiled, genuinely pleased to hear it. "I'm glad you've reconsidered. It would be a shame to miss such a momentous occasion."

She took a peek at him and smiled. "Are you a little nervous?"

"I'm not nervous…curious is more the word for it."

"I'm curious too." She grinned, her eyes twinkling excitedly. Brie left and shut the door behind her.

Brad smiled to himself.

He *knew* she couldn't resist a chance to film.

Brad spent the day at his place, playing with his whip in the basement of his new home. His backyard was much too small and open, but the basement of this old home was huge and had uncharacteristically high ceilings—perfect for his brand of play, and the main reason he'd chosen this particular home above all the others in the area.

Practicing in the basement meant he didn't have to worry about scaring Miss Em or inviting the interest of nosy neighbors wanting to spy on him. This new arrangement proved particularly useful on this day, allowing him to work out his energy without attracting the interest of others.

He hoped Boa was ready for tonight. Brad wasn't planning on being gentle with the man. His main interest was to see how far he could push the sub's limits while keeping him in a state of sexual arousal. Naturally, Brad was going to make Boa take the bite of his whip completely naked so the audience could enjoy the sub's infamous asset.

He, however, would be barefoot and bare-chested, but donning loose yoga pants and tight briefs. Brad did not want his own asset to become a distraction tonight. He wanted all of the focus to be on his bullwhip and the sub experiencing its unique bite for the first time.

Brad chuckled to himself after a particularly powerful stroke hit the wooden pole. Boa had no idea what he was in for, but Brad was determined that the sub would tremble at his feet when he was done—begging for more.

The Haven was beginning to fill up before Brie even showed up. Brad had no idea so many people in the community had been hungry to observe a scene between the two men.

He was afraid Brie might cut and run when she saw the crowd, so he had Marquis keep an eye out for her. No way was Brad going to allow Brie to continue hiding away. She was still young and full of life, even if her circumstances were intensely difficult.

Marquis brought Brie directly to him. The girl looked like a scared rabbit, glancing around nervously as she stood before him. This was not the confident girl Brad knew, but tonight he would help her reconnect with that girl again.

"Mrs. Davis had second thoughts, but I've convinced her this is exactly where she needs to be," Marquis informed him.

"I couldn't agree more, Gray." Brad shook his hand, sincerely grateful Marquis had persuaded Brie to stay— the only one who could.

Brad took the camera equipment from Brie's hands, ignoring the panicked look on her face. Once he got her settled behind the lens of her camera she would be fine, he was sure of it.

"Normally I'd be doing this scene in the alcove, but due to the high interest in tonight's event and the fact you'll be filming, I've been given a temporary stage to work on." He walked her around it, showing Brie where he thought her best shots might be. "I've got the areas marked off so you won't have to worry about being crowded by the spectators."

"Okay," she answered meekly, a tone uncharacteristic of her.

"You need to be aware that Boa will be completely naked for this scene."

All of a sudden Brie seemed to perk up, and she smiled for the first time that night. "Oh my…"

"You'll have to be creative how you shoot this. I'm assuming that naked buttocks are acceptable, but we both know that he will be protruding a bit up front."

Brie giggled. "Quite a bit actually… That should make it a challenge." She stared at the stage with new appreciation for the difficulty of the shoot.

"Let me walk you through the scene so you can get a better idea how to handle this bugger." Brad gave her a wink. "By the way, that flower looks nice in your hair."

She touched the white petals lightly. "I wear it whenever I film. It's a gift from Tono."

"Tell me more," Brad encouraged, keeping Brie's attention focused so she would not dwell on the growing number of people gathering around them. Unbeknownst to Brie, he had invited several people from The Submissive Training Center specifically to be with her tonight— after her filming was complete.

Mistress Lou came up to Brad with Boa by her side.

"Headmaster, I would like to give my sub over to you formally just before you begin the scene."

"Certainly," Brad answered.

"Mistress Lou, do you mind if I film the exchange?" Brie piped in, a timid look on her face.

"Not at all, Mrs. Davis."

The Domme held her hand out to take Brie's and squeezed it firmly. "I am glad to see you in person. Boa and I have been distraught about Mr. Davis's condition, but equally concerned about you. Your strength is inspiring, but know we are here for you should you need us."

Brie blushed. "Thank you, I'll keep that in mind."

"I can bring a few meals to the hospital," Boa offered, giving her a hug after asking permission from his Mistress.

Brad noticed that Brie seemed to gain confidence from their exchange, and he was encouraged. He knew from personal experience that it was easy to forget the power of caring friends in the shadows of despair.

Thane had taught him that.

Brie gave Boa a genuine smile when she said, "That won't be necessary, Boa. Master Anderson has all my cooking needs covered."

"Still, if you should require a meal at any point, the offer remains open."

Brie smiled and leaned towards him, asking quietly, "Boa, how are you feeling about this scene tonight?"

He rubbed his hands together, a large grin on his face. "I can't wait to start."

"Good. I must leave you three so I can finish setting up," Brie informed them, heading back to her camera equipment.

"How is she really, Headmaster?" Mistress Lou asked.

"Better, now that she's here," he answered, purposely vague to honor Brie's desire for privacy concerning the situation. "Thane has made small improvements, which gives us all hope. I'm just trying to keep Brie's head above water in the interim."

Mistress Lou put her hand on his arm and said solemnly, "You are a fine man, Headmaster."

"Just trying to live up to the standards Thane set," he replied. He glanced at the sea of people, shocked that the place was packed on a Sunday night. For a moment he felt a twinge of nerves, but he shook them off. The one thing he was good at was focusing on the moment at hand. He had the ability to ignore everyone around him, concentrating solely on the sub and the whip in his hand.

Tonight would be no different—other than the large crowd, the camera, and the fact he was scening with a man.

No different at all…

"Are we almost ready to begin?" Mistress Lou asked.

Brad looked at the time and nodded. In a loud voice, he announced to the people gathered, "We have a unique circumstance because this is being filmed, so I will need everyone's cooperation. The doors will be locked and remain locked until the scene is over. No one will be allowed to enter or exit until I am finished."

There was excited chatter amongst the attendees.

He spoke up again, "Since we are filming, you are not allowed to cross the yellow line taped to the floor. Also, I ask that you take on the role of silent observers. You will be given permission to speak after the scene is complete and I have given the signal."

"Yes, Master!" a bunch of subbies cried together.

"Way to go, Master Anderson!" a deep voice called out from the back.

Brad could feel the rising excitement in the building—it was even giving him a bit of a rush.

Taking a deep breath, he turned to Brie. "Ready, Mrs. Davis?"

She raised her thumb up in answer.

Brad faced Mistress Lou, and she began, "Headmaster Anderson, I am presenting to you my sub, Boa. He is yours for the duration of the scene. You are free to use him as you see fit under the parameters we have set prior to tonight."

Mistress Lou then turned to Boa, placing her hand over his heart. "Boa, serve the Headmaster well. Make your Mistress proud tonight."

"Yes, Mistress," Boa said humbly, bowing to her and then to Brad.

When Mistress Lou stepped back, Brad commanded in an authoritative voice, "Boa, look me in the eye."

The sub obediently gazed into Brad's eyes.

"You will strip here, then walk up onto the stage and stand on the x in the center."

"Yes, Headmaster Anderson."

Brad grasped the man's strong jaw and shook his head slowly. "Tonight, you call me Master."

There were a few audible gasps from the audience.

Brad stared at the crowd sternly with a raised eyebrow. When they quieted, he looked back at Boa and commanded, "Strip."

The sub immediately answered, "Yes, Master."

The sound of that title coming from a decidedly baritone voice was different for Brad. He watched with interest as the sub rid himself of his clothes, exposing a muscular body and a shaft that rivaled his own.

"Ready yourself," Brad ordered.

Boa made his way onto the stage, all eyes glued on his incredibly toned body with muscles that rippled as he ascended the steps.

Brad removed his own shirt and handed it to an eager sub in the crowd. "Guard it with your life," he ordered with a wink.

She only nodded, obeying his request to keep silent.

Brad grabbed his whip and began climbing the stairs, giving Brie and her camera lens a sultry smirk on his way up.

The lights were dimmed so that now only he and Boa were the center of focus. The huge place was unnaturally quiet, his steps echoing loudly on the wooden floor of the stage.

He smiled to himself, imagining how good his whip would sound tonight.

Brad walked up to Boa, his eyes locked on the sub as he placed his hand on the man's naked shoulder. "I will ask a lot of you tonight but, as always, you can call your safeword."

"Challenge me," Boa answered.

"Oh, I will…"

He felt Boa shudder beneath his hand, and he glanced down to see that the idea of it had stirred the sub's excitement.

Brad moved away with a slight smile on his lips, letting the audience appreciate the magnificence that was Boa's naked manhood.

He walked over to a table that had been set aside with the needed items for the scene. He grabbed the leather wrist cuffs and moved back over to the center of the stage. As Brad secured the cuffs to his wrists, he told Boa, "I like to have my submissives subdued. I want them to understand how helpless they are."

"I appreciate that, Master."

A single chain had been perfectly measured and then hung from the metal rafters above. He turned Boa so that it would be a better angle for Brie, and lifted the sub's arms, attaching both cuffs to the chain.

He'd made sure the height of it would force Boa onto the balls of his feet. A far more challenging position for someone who was about to face the bite of his whip.

"Feel helpless yet?"

"Yes, Master."

Boa stood still, showing off his impressive calf muscles in that position.

Brad went back to the table and unfurled his whip for everyone to see. He smiled down at the audience, feeling in complete control of the moment.

Without warning, he cracked the whip to the right side of Boa's cheek. The sub grunted in surprise as a few audience members let out frightened yelps.

Brad didn't reprimand them; he wanted to startle the audience and set the tone of his dominance.

He slashed the whip through the air a second time, close enough to move the hair next to Boa's ear.

The sub, to his credit, remained still. However, Brad could see he was beginning to tense his back muscles.

"Relax, Boa. The only way you can experience my whip properly is to un-tense those muscles."

Boa took a deep breath and let it out slowly. Brad was glad to see the tension leave his body.

Brad would normally start a new sub with gentle lashings to help build them up to his more spirited strokes, but Boa was used to the whip under the hand of his Mistress.

It was Brad's intention to introduce Boa straight away to the uniqueness of his male touch. He let a hard lash strike against Boa's back and nodded in satisfaction when the sub groaned loudly, swaying slightly in his bindings.

"Another," he said, as he lashed in the opposite direction, leaving two raised marks on Boa's back.

Beads of sweat appeared on Boa's skin, letting Brad know the strength of his strokes was extremely challenging for the submissive.

"Color, Boa."

"Yellow, Master."

"Good, now I know the line I cannot cross with you."

Brad went for his buttocks next. He pulled back on the power of the lashings to bring an element of uncertainty. Would the next stroke be pleasing or hit with a sting so intense it would take the man's breath away?

When he felt Boa was ready, Brad let the volley begin, strike after strike up and down his back. Brad kept it up for quite some time, longer than he had in the past, wanting to set Boa up for a subspace he would not forget.

Brad finally slowed down and then stopped. He coiled his whip and approached the sub. The man's back was drenched in sweat and his muscles were twitching of their own accord.

Brad placed his hand on Boa's shoulder and asked, "Are you flying yet?"

"So close, Master," Boa panted gruffly.

"Just a few more licks and then I set you to flight."

Boa turned his head toward Brad. "This is everything I hoped it would be."

"I'm not done yet," Brad whispered in his ear.

Brad wiped the sweat from his brow as he walked back into position. This was a challenging session for him as well. The exertion required was considerable, but he appreciated the challenge Boa represented. It had been a long time since he'd sweated so profusely.

Brad surprised the sub with gentle licks, first over his entire back and then lower and lower to his toned ass cheeks. For the first time, he heard the man moan, his skin suddenly covered in goosebumps.

Interesting...

The man was more stimulated when the strokes were light.

Who would have thought?

Knowing Boa's weakness, Brad tickled his back with the whip, surprising the sub with random strokes every now and then that stung. Keeping the man on his toes both figuratively and literally.

Finally, Boa could take no more and threw his head back, filling the large room with his passionate cries.

There was an echo of that same sexual energy coming from the crowd that Brad picked up on. His cock responded to that energy, and there was little he could do about it. Rather than fight against it, Brad searched the crowd and spotted the girl clutching his shirt, a sub he knew to be available, and pointed to her. He nodded in the direction where he wanted her to kneel and wait for him.

Brad returned his attention to Boa.

It was his norm to unbind his subs at this point, fuck them hard, then cuddle afterward.

Brad could tell aftercare was definitely needed for this male sub after the scene. He'd sent Boa deep into subspace and it was his responsibility to bring the man back safely from it.

He approached Boa, who hung limply from the chains. Releasing a wrist, he brought the muscular arm down slowly to let the blood flow back in while he rubbed the indent on the skin left by the tight cuff. Brad did the same with the other wrist.

Taking a page from Tono's playbook, Brad wrapped his strong arms around Boa's chest afterward, bare skin touching bare skin.

"Relax in my arms," he commanded.

The burly submissive leaned back against him, sur-rendering to his masculine embrace. His body pressed into Brad's rigid shaft. It couldn't be helped. However, Brad didn't mind that the sub knew his state of arous-al—it gave a submissive a sense of accomplishment knowing the Dominant had enjoyed the scene.

The two stood on the stage, the entire club so silent one could hear a pin drop.

Brad began whispering to Boa, sharing his personal impressions of their power exchange. Boa only nodded, slowly coming down from his sub-high.

It was a uniquely intimate moment that surprised Brad. He realized the gender of the sub hadn't mattered in the end. It was the spirit of the power exchange that made a scene pleasurable for him.

Would he consider doing such a thing again? Maybe...

When Brad felt Boa was ready, he released his hold and commanded the sub kneel where he stood. Boa moved sluggishly as he struggled to obey. Brad walked around and placed his hand on Boa's head. "You have served me well tonight."

"Thank you, Master," Boa replied hoarsely.

Brad then called Mistress Lou to join him on stage.

"Thank you for the use of your sub tonight, Mistress Lou."

The tiny woman smiled up at Brad, a glint in her eye. "It was an honor to watch you play with him, Headmaster."

"The honor was mine."

The Mistress helped Boa to his feet and guided him down the steps, the man still feeling the aftereffects of the sub-high he'd just experienced.

Brad faced the crowd, his cock hard and ready to dominate female flesh. He took a curt bow and the room burst in applause. Rather than bask in it, he descended the stairs and went straight for the kneeling submissive, who was still holding his shirt.

He placed his hand on her head. "Stand and serve me."

The girl looked up at him with eyes glowing with desire. "It's my pleasure, Master."

Brad led her to a nearby alcove where he released his passion on her. Her cries echoed throughout the building, adding a final emphasis to the scene.

He was covered in sweat when he finally met back up with Brie. "How was it?"

She lowered her eyes when she answered, "I am glad I was here to record it, and that I brought two towels."

He grinned, liking her answer. "Did you get good footage for the film then?"

"Most of it is unusable," she said, smiling. "However, I think I can string together enough clips to make an intriguing piece. But I will give you the unedited version so you can enjoy the brilliance of tonight's session. Truly a masterpiece of masculinity."

He chuckled, pleased that Brie had enjoyed it.

Brad gestured to Captain and Candy when Brie began packing up her equipment. They quickly made their way through the crowd over to Brie.

"Well, look who's here," Brad announced.

Brie looked up, and surprised him when she started to cry once she saw the couple.

Candy instantly went over and hugged her. "It's okay."

Brie quickly pulled herself together, wiping away the tears. "It's just that when I saw you, I instantly went back to that moment—all the fear and pain of that night."

Captain put his hand on her shoulder firmly. "There is no reason to revisit old feelings, Mrs. Davis. It's not the reason we came."

She nodded. "I owe you so much for how you handled the situation that night."

"You owe us nothing," Captain assured her.

Candy hugged her again. "We were grateful we could be there for you, Brie."

"Well, you both helped me survive that night…I will never forget it."

Marquis moved up to the group with Celestia by his side.

"We have something for you, Brie," Celestia gushed excitedly.

Brie smiled at her and waited as Marquis produced the item he was hiding behind his back.

As soon as she saw it, however, Brie burst into a fresh set of tears. "It's my parents' clock!"

She grabbed onto it with both hands, tears flowing down her cheeks. "I needed this," she sobbed between breaths. "Oh, my heart needed this…"

"I knew it was important to you," Marquis stated quietly.

"More than you can ever know."

Brad had been asked on several occasions by others in the community why Brie's parents hadn't come to her side after the crash. Most assumed there was a rift between them. What they didn't know, and he couldn't tell them, was that Brie had purposely pushed them away. She was terrified of her father finding out about the allegations Lilly had made. The last thing she wanted was for her father to side against Sir. So rather than suffer that possibility, she'd pushed her parents away, leaving her family hurt and at a loss.

Brad watched the way Brie hugged the monstrous glass clock. He realized when the plane went down, the series of events that followed had stolen everything of value from Brie. She'd been left dangling alone over the precipice.

Baron came up behind her. "Hey, kitten, it's good to see you out and about."

She turned her head toward him, not saying a word but nodding tearfully, still clutching the clock.

The dark Dom understood her pain on a level the others could not, and placed his arms around her, fortifying Brie with his strength—no words necessary between them.

Brie might be dangling over a dark precipice, but now she had the physical support of friends to strengthen her. Even through her tears, Brad could tell she was happy.

She'd needed this night to reconnect and remember the woman she once was—and would be again.

Second Strike

B rad was glad that the night at The Haven had inspired Brie to reach out to her girlfriends. Both had been fairly nonexistent since the crash. He wasn't sure if Brie had pushed them away as well, but it'd weighed heavily on him knowing how close Brie was with Lea, and how much Mary depended on Brie.

Girl power was its own unique entity.

He heard Brie talking to Lea while he was preparing the night's meal.

"Hey, girl, I've been thinking about you."

After a long pause, while listening to Lea's answer, Brie replied, "Are you sure everything's fine? You don't sound like yourself."

Apparently Lea changed the subject, because Brie immediately said, "I don't know what's going on with Mary, do you? I haven't heard a word from her."

Brie then giggled and confessed, "Well, I did accidentally spill the beans to Captain that she was struggling. I wonder if that has anything to do with her silence. If Mary's going to be that petty, especially after what's happened with Sir, then she can freakin' jump in a lake for all I care."

Lea must have cracked a joke because Brie started laughing and exclaimed, "Boo...that was terrible!"

Listening to the girl's laughter gave Brad a profound sense of peace. There was something exceedingly pleasant about listening to her giggle like a kid.

But that soon changed when Brie asked, "Seriously, Lea...I get the feeling something's up. Something that you're not telling me."

There was a long silence and then he heard Brie cry, "Oh no... I was afraid that would happen. How is she handling it?"

He peeked out from the kitchen and saw Brie shaking her head as she murmured into the phone, "I don't know what to say, girlfriend."

Brad could hear loud sobs coming from Brie's phone. Obviously, things were not well for Lea.

"Of course I understand, but I wish you would have told me. I'm still your BFF, you know—through thick and thin. Oh, Lea..."

Brad went back to his meal preparations, but he had the ominous feeling that instead of Brie benefitting from girl power, she was being given a new burden to carry. One that Lea had wanted to protect her from.

He more fully appreciated that there were times when silence was an act of caring. Sometimes keeping quiet was a gift of self-sacrifice to protect someone you loved from suffering further.

Brad made a mental note to call Samantha to find out what was wrong with Lea. They'd all grown close up in Colorado at The Denver Academy. Just because the miles separated them didn't mean he'd stopped caring. If needed, he could offer Lea a position at The Submissive Training Center if Samantha agreed it might help.

When Brie eventually got off the phone, Brad called her to the dinner table. "So things are not going well for Ms. Taylor, I take it?"

Brie sighed before answering. "I really hate to do this to you, but I promised Lea not to say anything."

Brad shook his head. "Seems to be the story of my life these days."

She reached out to squeeze his hand. "Your support and friendship have meant the world to me, Master Anderson. You've been my rock in the storm. Never doubt my admiration and appreciation for you. My silence is in no way reflective of how I feel."

"I understand, young Brie."

"Good," she said, squeezing his hand tighter. "Because I would be lost without you."

Brad didn't find out about Lilly's hijacking of Brie until after the incident.

He was working at the Training Center trying to catch up when his phone rang.

"Master Anderson," Brie cried, panic coloring her voice, "could you come to the hospital...now?"

"What's wrong?" Brad couldn't breathe while waiting for her answer, expecting to hear that Thane was dead.

"It's Lilly."

It was a relief to hear it, but he understood the seriousness of the situation. "Have the police been called? Are you at the hospital now?"

"Yes…"

"I'll be there as soon as I can. Stay put, don't you dare move." Brad sped through the streets, daring the cops to try to catch up with him.

Brad was grateful when he saw Nurse Abby on his way in. "What happened? How the hell did Lilly get past security?"

She shook her head. "It didn't happen here, Mr. Anderson. I'll go get Mrs. Davis so she can explain it herself."

Brad stopped her before she left to get Brie. "How is she, Abby?"

"Not well," the nurse answered, disappearing into the ICU.

When Brie walked out, her frightened expression and tear-stained face gutted him. He'd failed to protect her—again.

"What happened?"

"Lilly cornered me at the café down the street. I wasn't prepared…"

He immediately grabbed her, crushing her in his arms. "I can't believe she dared to show her face."

"I knew she would try something. I mean, I haven't heard from her in over a week and she hasn't tried to call me. I should have been better prepared."

"Lilly is seriously irrational, no one can predict her actions. What did the police tell you?"

"They are actively looking for her but, until she's apprehended, I won't feel safe. Lilly is smart, Master Anderson. She must have been stalking me to know that I go to that café occasionally for lunch. I never go anywhere else other than straight home. I figured I was safe with it being so close to the hospital." She shook her head, looking frightened. "I don't know what to do."

"You won't leave here alone again, that's all there is to it. We won't give her the opportunity to corner you a third time."

She nodded listlessly, obviously still in shock.

"I haven't even asked yet. What the hell happened?"

Brie's eyes flashed with fear. "I think she will really go through with it. She's going to destroy us."

"How?"

Brie buried her head in his chest. "I can't tell you."

"I'm really getting fucking tired of being left in the dark here. As Thane's friend and your caretaker, I *demand* to know what the hell is going on."

Seeing the disturbed glances from the hospital staff and patients, Brad escorted Brie to one of the private rooms reserved for grieving families.

He sat her down and apologized. "I'm sorry I caused a scene back there, but I am going ape-shit, Brie. That crazy witch is out to get you and unless I know why, how the fuck am I supposed to protect you?"

Brie stared up at him, her honey-colored eyes clouded with fear. "If I tell you, it may change how you think of Sir. I don't want that to happen. And Mr. Thompson said—"

"I don't give a rat's ass what the lawyer said."

Brie looked down at her hands, wringing them nervously.

Brad gave her time. He understood he was asking her to break the confidence she'd guarded so closely, one that she feared would permanently ruin his relationship with Thane.

What the fuck? That would never happen.

Finally, after much contemplation, Brie blurted, "Lilly's pregnant."

Brad shook his head, those words not computing in his brain. "What?"

She sighed, her voice quaking when she explained, "Lilly's pregnant and she's claiming it's Thane's child."

He sat back in his chair, completely stunned.

"She told me she has the genetic test to prove it."

"Holy fucking hell…"

Brie's bottom lip trembled when she confessed, "The scary thing is… she's far enough along for it to be true, and Sir never could remember what happened that night."

Brad growled angrily. "I don't care how drunk Thane got, he would *never* do such a thing. Why would you even entertain the idea?"

"I never told anyone this, but something terrible happened to Lilly. When she accused Sir, I definitely got the impression she'd been legitimately traumatized."

"So why did she come to you with this now?"

Brie looked down at her lap. "She wants half of Sir's money to keep quiet. She says she's doing it for the child's sake."

"Blackmail…" he snarled.

"Mr. Thompson told me she was threatening to blackmail Sir just before the crash." Brie added accusingly, "And he kept that from me. I suspect he even tore up the evidence in front of my eyes, telling me it didn't concern me. Why would he do that, Master Anderson?"

"I can't speak for Thane's actions, but he must have had a legitimate reason for keeping silent."

Brie slumped in her chair. "So now I'm faced with giving in to her demands and saving his name. Or doing nothing, and watching as she engages the press and ruins everything."

"Let her!" he roared. "She's a lying witch."

Brie shook her head. "If she does that, Sir's reputation will be forfeit even *if* she is lying. It would be exactly the same as what happened to his father."

"Damn, you're right about that," Brad growled, the ugly truth finally sinking in.

"I didn't believe her because she hasn't filed charges against Sir, but when I confronted her about it, Lilly claimed it was to protect the child's future." Brie looked at him sadly. "A child doesn't deserve to be known for the sins of the father."

"Yes, but why is she blackmailing you?"

"She wants the money to support her baby, since she claims Sir is financially responsible for a child he refuses to acknowledge." Brie sighed heavily. "But I also go back to that night when she seemed so distraught. I can't explain what happened to her—but it was something traumatic. She couldn't have faked that. And for the life of me, I can't fathom why Lilly would destroy ties to Sir by lying about this. None of it makes sense."

"Think about all the greenbacks and who her mother is—that should be explanation enough," Brad snarled.

"I've been doing what you said. I am trusting Sir and assuming that Lilly is lying—even though Sir couldn't remember anything about that night in China."

"As you should."

"Still I need to have a plan of action if the worst happens." She paused for a moment. "I must be ready for the press if she goes through with this, but…" Her voice broke when she whispered, "After what happened with Lilly today, I feel as if I'm about to shatter into a million pieces."

Brad gathered her in his arms, holding her so tight she could barely breathe. He felt her eventually relax, the restrictive embrace bringing comfort to her.

"Master Anderson," she mumbled against his chest, "when Lilly confronted me today, she was full of such rage. She sat down in the booth and grabbed my hand as if we were longtime friends, speaking to me in a calm, soothing voice so as not to attract attention as she demanded I get her the money. But when I looked into her eyes…it was like looking into the eyes of a demon." She snuggled against him. "I'm scared. I'm afraid she will do more than just talk to the press if I don't give her what she wants."

"Now that I understand what's happening, there is no reason to be afraid anymore. I *will* protect you from that witch no matter what it takes."

Brie drifted into the bedroom when they returned to the apartment, and came back a short time later with a leather journal in her hand. She looked at Brad nervously. "This is Sir's journal, the one he kept for me while he was in China. The only thing is...he never shared it."

They both looked at the unopened ledger.

"By my way of thinking, I have permission to read it because it was written specifically to me."

Brad nodded, saying nothing.

"I feel like this may be a Pandora's box. Yet, I'm compelled to open it. We both journaled while we were apart. It was Sir's idea. He said it would help with the separation and bring us closer together once we were reunited."

"Did you talk with him about it?"

"Only once, and he pretty much brushed it aside, saying it was old news. I poured my heart into my journal and he read mine. Don't you think it's only fair that I should read his—especially when it pertains to the night in question?"

Brad looked warily at the journal. "While I agree, I am unsure if it's wise. There must have been a reason he didn't share it with you."

"I need to know."

"It's your decision to make. I cannot advise you either way."

Brad got up to leave, wanting to give her privacy.

"Please don't go, Master Anderson. If it is good news, I'll want to share it with you, and if it is not, I will need your support."

He sat down opposite Brie. Cayenne jumped up on

his shoulder and purred when he scratched under her chin. "We are here for you."

Brie opened up the journal and started from the beginning. After she had read the first entry, she looked up at him with tears in her eyes. "It's like he's right here beside me. I hear his voice reading these words." Brie wiped away a stray tear that fell. "He really missed me that first night."

As she continued reading, her brows furrowed. She stopped partway through and looked up at him. "I didn't appreciate just how devastated Sir was when Lilly claimed her mother had opened her eyes. I knew it troubled him, but to see it written out in his own words... Sir wanted it to be true for his sister's sake, but he feared what it would do to him—and to us—if Ruth recovered." Brie shook her head, stroking the page. "I wish I could have been there for him."

"You were in spirit."

She said in the barest of whispers, "I don't think it was enough." Brie stared at the page. "He needed me, Master Anderson, but he put Faelan before himself."

Brie continued reading on and started shaking her head. She flipped the page back and forth before mumbling, "It's just like Sir said. He was so consistent recording each day, but there is nothing written on that night. In fact..." She put her finger on the date on the upper left. "He didn't write anything for the next two days."

She sighed anxiously. "His handwriting looks shaky and different in this next entry. I'm afraid to read what comes next."

"You can still walk away, young Brie."

She looked up at him and shook her head. "No, I can't."

With trembling hands, Brie lifted the journal up to continue reading. Brad watched her face, waiting for any telltale signs alerting him to whether Thane's own words would defend or condemn him.

What he saw instead was a look of confusion as she read through it.

Finally, Brie looked up from the journal and told him, "I don't understand...but you'll have to hear it in context."

Brad leaned forward, hoping to glean from Thane's words what Brie needed to hear. She began reading aloud starting back on the previous page. "Babygirl, my head still isn't right. I can't think, I can't eat, and my body won't stop shaking. I feel as if I've been poisoned but, if so, that would be of my own doing. It was meant as a simple night of celebration at Lilly's insistence. Even I got caught up in her enthusiasm, partially hoping for her sake she was right about Mother's recovery so I wouldn't have to see the devastation in her eyes when the scan came back proving the woman was brain dead.

"You know I don't overindulge, but we did drink several concoctions at a local bar. How much and what they were, I can't say. The night quickly became a blur. I felt like a frat boy when I woke up in my hotel room the next day unaware how I had gotten there. More disturbing was the fact my clothes were dirty and torn. Again...I have no recollection why.

"Seeing my sorry condition, I stumbled to Lilly's

room to check on her. She was slow to answer and in the same disheveled state. When I asked her about it, she only shook her head. It seemed her memory was as compromised as mine.

"I wasn't able to go to the hospital that day, feeling too sick to leave my bed. Lilly told me she'd been well enough by the afternoon to visit Mother and saw her eyelids flutter. Her false hope struck me the wrong way.

"I guess it may have been the aftereffects of alcohol that caused me to lash out, but whatever the case, I made the girl cry when I told her Mother would never recover because she's already dead. I didn't care that she refused to speak to me the rest of the day. I needed time alone to recover.

"That's when the dreams started. I was awakened time and time again by nightmares littered with disturbing images and unholy screams. It's been two days, and I've still been unable to rest—and the shaking won't stop.

"Lilly is overly concerned, and has become highly attentive, trying to force herbal remedies and local soups down my throat. It grates on my nerves and I keep sending her away.

"I want no one near me but you. However, I don't trust myself."

Brie choked out the last few words. "Babygirl, I seriously don't know what's wrong with me. I feel as if I have entered a black hole I won't return from."

Brie put down the journal. "He only has one other entry after that." Her lips trembled when she said, "But what he says doesn't make any sense and is extremely hurtful."

She slid the journal over to Brad, explaining, "I can't read it out loud."

Brad looked down at the page; the writing looked dark and ragged, as if written with great force.

Dear Miss Bennett,

Your delay in coming to me speaks volumes. After much deliberation and discussion, I have come to the conclusion that you are a whore and cannot be trusted.

The words shocked Brad. They were uncharacteristic of Thane and he told her, "There is no way he wrote this."

Brie shook her head. "I remember when I finally arrived in China, Sir was not happy to see me. I felt his rage toward me, but had no idea of the reason for it." Her eyes revealed unspoken fears.

Brad growled under his breath. "What the fuck happened there…"

"I don't know, but I remember Lilly was particularly displeased to see me."

Brad picked up the journal and read through it again. His anger growing with every word—a few key things standing out.

"Thane states that Lilly acted as if she couldn't remember what happened that night. That's huge because she claimed otherwise."

Brie nodded her agreement.

"Also, Thane admits she was angry about his statement concerning their mother, but was still willing to help him through his sickness—that she tried to care for him even though he turned her away repeatedly. That doesn't make sense for a woman who alleges he was her attacker."

Brie nodded again, but it was obvious that the shock of the last entry was still ringing in her head. He understood, and addressed it next.

"Thane's final entry is not his thoughts, and the fact he used the word 'discussion' is telling. I assume he must have spoken with Lilly, and I'm convinced she put those ideas in his head."

Brie whimpered. "But why would Sir listen to her?"

"I can't say, but we know his health was compromised at the time based on his journal entries. Seeing how it all played out, including her stealing his cell phone, I'm convinced she was plotting against you personally."

He saw her shudder and put a protective arm around her. "I won't let her touch you, young Brie."

Brad ordered out that night. Brie seemed too fragile to leave her alone to her thoughts even for a minute. Instead of cooking another soup, he spent the night with her watching Cayenne destroy another feathery toy while Shadow watched from the safety of Brie's lap.

It seemed the dark beast understood the seriousness of Brie's fragile mental state and refused to leave her side even when Brad sidled up next to her. Brad admired the cat for it and was grateful fate had seen fit to bring the unusual creature to Brie in this time of need.

When it finally came time to sleep, he watched the

girl retire to her bedroom with both cats following behind her. He headed to the guest bedroom and called Marquis, only informing him that he would be absent for another day while he figured out how best to handle the situation.

"Is there anything I can do?" Marquis asked.

"You're a praying man, right?"

"Yes."

"Pray that Brie survives a new complication that has arisen and that justice is served. Our former student is teetering on the edge, and I'm unsure how best to help her."

"You are doing the right thing by being a physical presence. There are times when that is all that is required. However, both Celestia and I will pray for Mrs. Davis, and I will inform the panel of your continued absence."

"I'm not making a good impression as Headmaster, am I?"

"As a matter of fact, you are. Your care of Mrs. Davis is an example to the students that being an active part of the community is where you experience the true strength of our BDSM community."

"You always have good insights, Gray. I'm glad to know you."

"I feel the same, Headmaster Anderson. Keep me abreast of what's happening, and let me know where I can help."

"Will do."

Brad got undressed afterward. He preferred to wear nothing to bed because he didn't care for the restrictive feel of clothing when he slept. However, when he was a guest in someone's home, he always covered up from the waist down to avoid awkward moments.

It was a good thing too, because he woke up to find young Brie beside his bed. He heard her soft gasps and realized she was crying in the dark.

"What's going on?"

"I had a dream."

"There's no need to cry, you're awake now."

Her voice quavered in the darkness. "I saw him…"

"Who?"

"Sir."

Brad was groggy after being awakened from a deep sleep and needed a second to get his wits about him. He sat up in bed and turned on the lamp, patting the bed.

She lay down next to him, her eyes shining with tears. "Sir looked just like that night when he left for the plane…"

Brad put one arm around her. "I'm sorry."

"No, you don't understand. Sir spoke to me."

Still not quite awake, he muttered, "What?"

"I'm not sure what he meant, because he only said one word—*Don't*. His plea was so haunting that it woke me out of a deep sleep."

"It was just a dream, young Brie. Don't concern yourself."

Brie shook her head, acting out the scene as she explained it to him. She gently cradled Brad's jaw in her small hand. "Sir touched my cheek like this and looked deep into my eyes…" She drew closer to Brad so they were only inches apart. "And he said 'Don't' just once."

"Then he disappeared," she cried, pulling away from him. "It seemed so real to me. I *felt* his touch. It was as if Sir was reaching out to me in my sleep."

Although Brad wasn't into dream interpretation, he suggested, "Maybe Thane can feel your conflict."

She sucked in her breath. "That's it... I should never have doubted him. Sir *knows* I have been questioning everything that's happened."

A fresh set of tears began, and all Brad could do was hold her as she worked through the grief his words had caused.

Taking command of her errant thoughts, Brad insisted, "If you'd acted like a mindless puppet, questioning nothing, *then* Thane would have reason to be upset. You've been loyal to him through all of this despite the circumstances. I'm proud of you, and he would be too. Now stop with the tears. I told you I can't handle crying."

He continued to hold her while she forced herself to calm down. "I know this sounds strange, but it hurt so good seeing him again, Master Anderson," she shared, her voice ragged with emotion. "I feel like I was really with Sir tonight."

"Then hold on to that feeling. You can use that dream as encouragement. Don't give up."

"Don't give up..." she said, suddenly smiling. "*That's* what he meant." She settled into his arms and asked him, "Do you know what I ended up doing with my parents' clock, Master Anderson?"

"No clue. Why don't you tell me?"

"I put it near his bed so he could hear the ticking of

the clock and I told him, 'Every second that ticks by is one less second apart. Hold on to that sound, and fight to come back to me.'"

Brad cleared his throat, forcing himself not to get emotional. "That's a good use of the clock."

She snuggled up against him. "I thought so too."

Brad was appreciative that Nurse Abby met him when he came to collect Brie. She allowed him to enter Intensive Care, explaining, "I put you down as Mr. Davis's adopted brother."

He nodded his approval. "Thane would agree with that."

She gestured toward the room farthest to the left. "She's in there."

Brad walked toward it, looking through the glass that acted as a transparent wall. He stopped when he saw Brie. He could hear faintest sound of music drifting from the room, and instantly recognized the dubstep song by Rain Man called *Bring Back the Summer*.

Brie was swaying to the music, facing Thane's bed as if he were her dance partner. Her movements were expressive and passionate as she poured out her soul in her movements.

Tears welled in Brad's eyes as he watched her twirl with her hands close to her chest while the haunting lyrics "I never, I never want another…" played in the background, then Brie made the motions of calling

Thane back with tears running down her cheeks as the words "Come back, come back to me, my lover..." floated in the air.

Thane just lay there, eyes open but oblivious to her heartfelt pleas.

Brad had to swallow back the tender emotion her dance inspired. The love Brie had for Thane was powerful and priceless. It seemed cruel that such devotion wasn't rewarded by Fate.

He turned to Abby and quickly explained, "I need to get something before I disturb her."

Brad headed back to his truck, determined to put a smile on Brie's tear-stained face. He drove to the flower shop close to The Submissive Training Center where he knew the owner personally. Brad asked Mabel to make a special bouquet.

"Make it big. No, jaw-droppingly *huge*," he instructed. "I want the woman to know how much I admire her."

"Is this for a new love interest?" Mabel asked with a smile. "I only ask so I can make sure the arrangement meets the mood you're trying to set."

Brad shook his head. "No, no...it's for a friend who really could use a smile right now."

"Very well." With graceful, yet meticulous hands, Mabel took simple flowers and created a living piece of art before his eyes. When she was done, Mabel stood back and grinned.

"What do you think, Master Anderson?"

Brad stared at the tall, slim arrangement of purple, yellow, and cream flowers with magnificent Birds of Paradise scattered artfully throughout.

"It's a showstopper, Mabel."

"Do you think your lady friend will like it?"

"She'll be absolutely blown away by this." Brad handed her an extra-generous tip, wanting to show appreciation for the skill of the flower artisan.

"I can't accept this," she protested.

He smiled. "I insist. I can't wait to see the look on Brie's face when she beholds this creation."

Master Anderson struggled getting the large arrangement in his truck without damaging the delicate flowers. He carefully buckled the vase in.

Turning on some deep bass on his stereo, he made his way back to the hospital. While he was driving, he came to the realization that he wasn't doing it for Thane—or even for Brie. Truthfully, this gesture was purely selfish on his part. If he could get Brie to smile, he'd be giving a finger to the bitch called Fate.

He saw too late what was waiting for him when he crested the hill overlooking the hospital. A bent, little old lady in a housecoat was standing in the middle of the road for no apparent reason. Brad slammed on his brakes but knew impact was inevitable. Without giving a second thought, he swerved to avoid hitting the old woman, heading for the ditch on the side of the road.

"Oh fuck…"

The truck pitched into a roll. He knew, without a doubt, it was going to end badly for him and his Chevy.

His very last thought before everything went black was of Shey Allen.

Brad woke up in a white, sterile room and found himself tucked in crisp linen sheets. He turned his head and was surprised to see a familiar face. "Is that you, Nurse Abby?"

"Oh good, you're awake. Mrs. Davis is going to be so relieved. I thought she was going to have a total breakdown when she heard you'd been admitted to the emergency room."

"The old woman?"

"She's fine, as is the turtle she was trying to save."

Brad shook his head. "Well, at least my truck didn't die for nothin'."

Abby looked at his leg, frowning sadly. "You aren't going to be driving anytime soon, I'm afraid."

"Damn, this really fucks things up. Excuse my language," he amended quickly.

"No need to apologize," Abby said, waving away his comment. "All of the nursing staff are concerned for you. We're here however you need us."

He shook his head. "Don't worry about me, it's Mrs. Davis who needs support."

"Well, she's going to have to live without yours for a bit. With your right leg out of commission, you won't be up and about for a while, but at least it was a clean break."

Knowing that Lilly was still out there, Brad couldn't leave Brie alone and defenseless—not for one second.

"I need to make a call."

Abby handed him the portable phone sitting on the hospital tray by his bed.

He stared at it for a while, unsure who to call.

The first person who came to mind was Rytsar Durov. Although he hadn't recently heard from the man, he was a sound choice. However, Brad was unsure how the Russian would fare with a hurting Brie under his care. She already had a strong sexual bond with the man. It would be extremely easy for Rytsar to fall into the trap of wanting to comfort the girl, thereby allowing the emotional bond between them to take on new life. The Russian was a passionate man by nature.

Although Rytsar was an honorable Dom, this precarious balance had been hard enough on Brad, and made him cautious about his decision. It wasn't so much that Brad didn't trust Rytsar as much as he felt putting the two together would only set them up for failure.

For Brad there was really only one man who could provide Brie with the guidance, love, and calming support she needed—and still be trusted to keep his focus.

"Hey, Nosaka…"

Brad explained the entire situation, excluding the details behind Lilly's threat, letting the Kinbaku master know just how serious things were for Brie.

"There is no one else she needs more right now than you."

"Why do you say that?"

"I've noticed she's taken to wearing the white orchid in her hair each day. She strokes it obsessively when she thinks no one is watching. She is not well, Nosaka."

While the man was digesting that news, Master Anderson added, "Lilly poses a serious threat to Brie. Is there any way you can take a flight out today? I'm not kidding when I say time is of the essence."

Tono Nosaka did not hesitate for a second. "I will be there as soon as possible."

Brad let out a sigh of relief. "If anything happened to Brie, I'm afraid I'd completely lose it. She's in a fragile state right now and could shatter at any moment."

"I will make the necessary arrangements. Should I head to the hospital when I arrive?"

"No, go directly to the apartment. I'll call ahead so the front desk will be expecting you. Everyone's on high alert because of Lilly's actions."

"What's going on?"

"I'll let Brie give you the details when she sees you."

"How long I should plan on staying then?"

"Once I'm back on my feet, I can take over. Maybe a couple of weeks."

Abby tsked at him.

"I stand corrected. The nurse is telling me it might be a bit longer."

"Fine. I will seek out someone to temporarily care for your place while I join you in LA."

"Sorry about the inconvenience."

"Not an issue. That's what family is for."

"You're a good egg, Nosaka."

"Brie's well-being is of utmost importance. I've felt unsettled for quite some time, but was told by Sir Davis's aunt that there was no need for concern."

"That came as a direct order from Brie. She didn't

want anyone worrying about her."

"It will actually be a relief to see her in person," he admitted. "Know that I'm glad to help in any way while Sir Davis recovers."

"I'm warning you, Nosaka, it's not looking good."

"It will eventually, Master Anderson. There are always calm seas after a tempest."

"See? Now that's the kind of shit Brie could use."

"I help where I can."

"I have a piece of advice for you after having looked after Brie myself. She's a hurting unit right now. The pain is just under the surface and is easy to read even though she puts on a strong front. I don't mean to offend you when I say this, but it's imperative to comfort her without being overly comforting. Especially considering your history together. Do you get what I'm saying?"

"I do, Master Anderson. I understand fully what is being asked of me. Fortunately, I have been down this road with her when I was asked to take on the role as her temporary Master by Sir Davis when he was away on business."

"That's why I called you. If Thane trusted you then, I know I can trust you now." He paused for a moment. "It's just that I found the situation more challenging than I thought it would be. You can't help but want to wrap that little girl in your arms and take all the pain away."

"Knowing the challenge is there makes it easier to avoid," Nosaka stated.

"Exactly. I resorted to humor and cooking soup to circumvent the issue whenever it arose. I don't know what your tools are, but they worked for me."

"I assure you I will be thoughtful in my interactions with her, Master Anderson. I desire to increase her harmony and peace, not distract from it."

"That's what she needs—along with your protection. Lilly is unbalanced."

"I will keep Brie safe in both mind and body, Master Anderson."

Brad believed Nosaka and felt good after hanging up. The Asian Dom was an uncommon man with the ability to center those around him.

"Hell, even I could use his brand of shit," he confessed to Nurse Abby as he handed her the phone. "You're going to like this Nosaka person, I guarantee it."

She smiled as she finished up with him, pushing the tray next to his bed before she left.

Brad stared long and hard at the phone sitting there, thinking back on his accident.

Damn...to call her now would only invite complication into his already complex life. He didn't need Shey's pity, but he yearned to hear her voice.

"Oh, what the hell... You only live once."

Unexpected Visit

B rad heard a soft rapping on the door.

"Just leave it on the doorstep, whatever it is," he called out, tired of getting fruit baskets from the staff and administration at The Center. He understood it was meant as a kind gesture, but what was he going to do with all that rotting fruit? He was only one man, for goodness sake.

To his irritation, the rapping continued. He was about to yell, "Go the fuck away!" when he noticed Cayenne walk up to the door.

"So you know this person..." Brad stated with interest as he grabbed his crutches and painfully pushed himself from the couch to head toward the door. "I'm coming, I'm coming," he grumbled.

He was slow to unlock the bolt, moving between the door and Cayenne to prevent her escape as he cracked the door.

His jaw dropped when he saw who it was.

The redhead smiled up at him shyly, wearing his black Stetson on her head. Her cheeks were flushed with a pleasant pink.

"Shey?"

She giggled lightly. "It's me, in the flesh."

He quickly ushered her inside, his mind not quite registering that the redhead was actually standing in front of him. "You didn't have to come, you know."

"Of course I did. As soon as you told me you were in an accident I started making plans to visit." She tentatively touched his shoulder. "But it looks like it wasn't only your truck that suffered in the crash. Why didn't you tell me you broke your leg?"

Brad laughed uncomfortably, shaken by the fact he'd felt chills when she touched him. "Don't mind me, I'll mend soon enough." Making his way back to the sofa using his crutches, he motioned Shey to sit. "What really brought you down here?"

The pink blush became more intense when she answered. "I finally did it. I took your advice and had a real talk with my parents."

Cayenne jumped on Shey's lap and began purring, so Brad reached out and scratched the feline's head as he continued to stare at Shey.

She's really here.

"After I explained that you were in an accident and how I felt about you, I was overwhelmed by my parents' response."

"What did they do?"

"They both practically pushed me out the door."

"Why?" he asked, chuckling.

"I guess they'd been worried I would remain a spinster forever."

"So all this time you've been worried about your parents, and they've been equally worried about you?"

She laughed. "I guess. They bought me a new car and told me in no uncertain terms that I need to fully explore California…" She paused, the pink shade of her blush suddenly turning red. Shey slumped on the couch as if she had something more she was embarrassed to tell him. Finally, she whispered, "As well as my relationship with you."

He had to hide the shit-eatin' grin that threatened to take over his face and answered simply, "I see."

Shey took a deep breath. "I hope I'm not being overly forward, coming here unannounced like this."

Brad smirked, ticking the brim of her hat. "Are you kidding me, Shey? I've been waiting for you to knock on this damn door ever since I left Vegas."

Her laughter filled the room, and she nodded with a pleased smile. "Good."

"So where are you staying?"

"I'm staying at a hotel nearby, but will be looking for a studio apartment once I get settled. Mr. Nyte hooked me up with a job out here."

"You could always stay here with me," Brad suggested. "Got a guest room just waiting for ya."

Her eyes widened, her face frozen in a look of complete shock.

"What? Did I say something wrong?"

Shey tilted her head. "I…mean, I know we got off to a quick start when you came to Vegas, but that's not normal for me."

He'd momentarily forgotten that she wasn't one of

his kinky friends who would think nothing of an offer to stay with him. "Look, I'm sorry, Shey. I definitely didn't mean to overstep with my offer. I want to take it as slowly as you want—even if that means no sex until six months down the road. In my eyes, it was a simple offer to a friend."

She swallowed hard. "Okay, because I'm not like the other girls you know. I'm kind of old-fashioned, despite what transpired between us that night."

He nodded. "I totally get that. You're looking for a strictly vanilla relationship."

She laughed. "Not exactly. I like the idea of exploring BDSM with you, but I want to be treated like your girlfriend, not a sub. At least not in the beginning."

He raised an eyebrow. "But you are open to the idea."

She shrugged with a coy smile. "Sure, if it's something I feel called to do."

"I respect that."

"The only thing I'm not sure about...and I still can't wrap my head around...is..." Her voice trailed off.

"Are you talking about what I do for a living?"

She took a deep breath. "Yes, that."

"Is it the fact I scene with my students or that I have intercourse during the sessions?"

"Both, if I'm completely honest. However, it's the latter that truly bothers me."

He stared at her perplexed. "Why have you come then, Shey? You know that's part of my job."

Her smile crumpled. "I don't know... I'm hoping you can convince me it's okay somehow."

Brad chuckled but shook his head slowly. "You're an old-fashioned girl—no amount of convincing on my part is going to change your heart."

Shey wiped away an unwanted tear. "I was afraid of that, but...I *had* to come see you, Brad. I have to at least try."

He held out his arms to her and she settled into his embrace. Kissing her gently, he murmured, "I'm glad you came."

Even though he was laid up with a bum leg, Brad still had to fulfill his responsibilities at The Center. Every night, Baron would make the drive to pick him up and take him to work.

"I hate that you have to do this," Brad complained. "I'm only like ten minutes away from the damn place."

Baron grinned at him. "Since you can't drive, it would take an hour or longer on those crutches."

Brad snarled. "I hate feeling like a helpless baby, but...thank you."

"Anytime, Headmaster."

Plans for the students' upcoming graduation was on the agenda for the meeting after class ended that night. Since the crash, Brad had headed all the sessions. However, Baron and Marquis had been forced to pick up the slack where physical training was concerned.

Tonight, Nosh had to be called in as Brad's replacement since a third trainer was needed for a unique scene planned for one of the pupils.

Brad was feeling restless just minutes before it was set to start, and quietly left to grab a glass of water. He smiled at the students as he passed, ignoring the sympathetic expressions on their faces. God, he couldn't wait to lose these damn crutches and rip the fucking cast from his leg.

He growled under his breath as he pulled out a bottled water from the fridge and took a long drink.

"What's wrong?" Mr. Gallant asked, walking into the trainer's lounge. "Nothing to do with the students, I trust."

"No, it's a personal issue I'm dealing with."

"Not with Mrs. Davis, I hope."

"No, Nosaka keeps in touch with me daily and says Brie is actually doing well—considering."

Mr. Gallant looked up at him with gentle but penetrating eyes. "What is it then?"

He let out a long sigh before confessing, "I haven't told anyone."

"Your confidence is safe with me," Mr. Gallant assured him.

"Well…I met a girl."

The teacher laughed. "How many disasters start with that very phrase?"

Brad grinned. "True enough, but in this case, she's not the problem. I am."

Mr. Gallant pulled out a seat for Brad and sat down on the seat next to it.

"I really should get back, Gallant."

"Will you be able to properly focus on the students?"

he asked.

Brad chuckled, knowing he could not, and sat down next to Mr. Gallant. "It's like this. I believe I've met the woman I'm meant to grow old with. Only catch—my new position. You see, this girl is pretty traditional and although she appreciates kink, she can't handle the idea of her man scening with other women, even if they are his students."

"I see," Mr. Gallant replied. "It seems like a reasonable request on her part. Your fidelity for hers."

Brad snorted. "Reasonable if I wasn't the Headmaster of The Submissive Training Center."

Mr. Gallant smiled kindly at Brad as he shared, "I've been here since the school opened more than twenty-five years ago."

"Wow, I had no idea."

"The point is, when I applied for the position of their main teacher, I was told that it was expected I would scene with students just as the trainers do."

Brad leaned in closer. "I never knew that."

"I wanted the job, but I had made a solemn vow to my beloved wife and would not compromise my marriage for this prestigious school. Therefore, I explained to the headmaster that I could not have any physical relations with the students, although I would dedicate my life to helping my pupils succeed."

"And you got the job," Brad stated in admiration.

"I did, without compromising myself or the relationship with my wife."

Brad leaned back. "It's a great story, Gallant, but that was more than twenty-five years ago. As headmaster, I have a set of rules I must follow and uphold. Personal engagement with the students is one of them."

Gallant smiled at him as if he were waiting for Brad to catch up with his line of thinking.

"What is it, Gallant? What am I missing?"

"All that is needed is a change in the requirements of your position."

"Are you suggesting I change the responsibilities of the headmaster?" Brad snorted in amusement, stating in an official tone, "From now on, the Headmaster is *not* allowed to have physical relations with students." He shook his head. "Right...no one would agree to that."

"The idea is not unfounded. It was actually suggested a few years ago when a certain headmaster 'compromised' one of the students at The Center."

"What? Did Master Coen suggest the change because of Thane?" Brad asked in surprise.

"No, it was Marquis Gray in fact. I believe if you were to make that suggestion now it would be well received and have the support of most of those on staff."

Brad shook his head in disbelief, a smile creeping across his face. "A headmaster who refuses to have intercourse with the students...who'd have thought?"

"Not any crazier than a teacher at The Center who doesn't, now is it?"

Brad laughed, looking down at his palms. "The power was always in my hands, I just didn't see it."

"Like Dorothy in the World of Oz," Mr. Gallant agreed.

Brad forced himself to his feet and leaned against

one crutch so he could shake hands with the respected teacher. "I think you may have just changed the course of my life, Mr. Gallant."

The small man smiled with a slight nod. "I would hate to lose a qualified Headmaster over something so trivial and easily fixed."

Brad invited Shey out for lunch the next day, taking her to a small French restaurant that was a five-minute hobble on crutches from his home—a little place Baron had introduced him to.

"Wow, I wasn't expecting to taste a piece of France in LA," Shey exclaimed, sitting in the chair he offered her.

The tiny restaurant was filled with authentic décor. The waitstaff, along with most of the customers, were chattering away in French.

"Wait until you taste the food, Shey. You'll think you have died and gone to heaven."

"What's the special occasion?" she asked.

"I have some news, Shey. I've made a decision about my job that may make you smile."

Instead of smiling, Shey looked horrified. "Please don't say you quit. I could never handle it if you lost your job because of me."

Brad looked at her warmly, touched that that was her first response. "No, I've worked too hard to walk away now."

She looked confused and asked, "What did you decide then?"

His grinned widened when he told her, "After receiving some sage advice from a well-respected colleague, I am changing the role of the Headmaster."

Shey's eyes lit up. "Go on..."

"The Headmaster will not be allowed to engage in intercourse with any of the students. The other trainers on the panel will be responsible for that physical aspect of the job."

"Can you do that?"

"I can, and I have."

Tears welled up in her eyes. "I can't believe you did that for me."

Brad took her hand. "I did it for *us*, Shey."

Her bottom lip trembled as the waiter served the wine and their first appetizer at the table.

Brad picked up one of the shells on the plate. "Have you ever had escargot?"

She shook her head, looking a little daunted.

"I think you will find them surprisingly tasty and tender." He speared the flesh dripping with sauce and put it to her lips.

Shey looked up at him with complete trust as she opened her mouth.

"Enjoy," he told her in a low, seductive growl.

Shey slowly chewed the bite. As she did so, Brad was pleased to see the surprise on her face.

"You like?"

After Shey had swallowed, she nodded. "I like it very much, but even more so because of the sexy way you fed it to me."

She picked up one of the snail shells and used the tiny fork to dig out the creature. Leaning over the small table, she put it to his lips. Brad slowly opened his mouth, looking at Shey the entire time. He groaned softly when he tasted the bite.

Shey's eyes were luminous as she watched his lips while he chewed. There was a reason escargot was considered an aphrodisiac.

When they were done teasing each other with the appetizer, he took a sip of his wine and explained, "Now, I will still be scening with these students. My expertise is the reason I was offered this position. I remember you mentioned that was also an issue for you."

Shey took his left hand in both of hers. "What you did makes me reconsider what I said before. I think if I were able to observe you working with your students, I would have a better understanding. However, I can say this without reservation—I trust you."

He leaned over and kissed her tenderly on the lips, mindful of where they were and the fact others were watching. However, had he been alone with Shey, he would have thrust his tongue between her lips and claimed that luscious mouth.

Throughout the meal, Brad noticed the way she kept sneaking glances at him as she ate, the subtle lick of her lips, the unconscious twirl of her hair. She wanted him, and he definitely wanted her.

As they walked back to his home after the meal, Brad broached the subject. "I know you said you are a traditional girl and you wanted to take it slow."

"Yes," she answered, looking up at him with a flirtatious smile.

"You can certainly set me straight if I am being too forward here," he stated, as he stopped in the middle of the sidewalk. Leaning against one crutch, he freed a hand so he could cradle her chin as he gazed deep into her ocean-blue eyes. "Shey Allen, I want to make love to you."

Brad shrugged after his declaration. "There, I said it." Grabbing onto his crutches, he continued hobbling down the street.

The two walked in silence for several minutes.

"Brad, I hear what you're saying. When I told you I wanted to take it slowly I was being serious…" Shey began.

He nodded, knowing she was trying to let him down gently.

"But the fact is, I'm desperate for you." She smiled more boldly. "If you weren't on crutches, I'd race you to your bedroom."

He threw back his head and laughed. "Hot damn, you're my kind of lady."

Shey went on to explain, "There are some aspects of our courtship I would like to keep traditional. Things like not moving in together until the time is right. Of course, my parents would prefer we wait to cohabitate until marriage, but it seems a little silly to me when we already," she cleared her throat and grinned, "know each other biblically."

Brad chuckled. "Yes, we certainly do."

"But I would still like to go on dates so we can get to

know each other like most couples do. There's no reason to rush this."

"I agree it would be healthy to treat our relationship as if we were just starting out." He lifted her hand to kiss it. "We *did* only have one night together."

"One incredible night," she purred.

"If things go well between us, Shey, I would like to eventually meet your parents and for you to meet mine. I haven't brought a girl home to them since high school. I know it weighs heavily on their hearts—the fact that I haven't found a partner yet."

"My parents have been similarly concerned about me."

"They sound a lot alike. Bet they would get along famously."

"Since we're being open, Brad, as far as my future goes, I have really simple desires. I'd just like to settle down in one place and have a bunch of kids. Seriously, I can't wait to be a mother."

Brad stopped abruptly but quickly regained his composure and kept hobbling.

Shey smiled up at him and teased, "What? Don't you want children?"

"I hadn't really considered it," he lied.

"I can just imagine you as a father. You'd be strict but funny. The kids would absolutely adore you."

Shey was talking as if she could already see the children walking beside them. It gave him the creeps and he shuddered.

Changing the subject, Brad told Shey, "With this bum leg, I'm not going to be able to make love to you the way I want. We'll have to improvise."

She raised her eyebrows at his suggestion. "And I look forward to seeing what that looks like."

Brad tightened his grip on the crutches, moving along at a much faster rate. "Race ya, darlin'."

This Moment

Once they were in his house, Shey told him to head to the couch. She then took his crutches from him and laid them on the coffee table, ordering him to take off his shirt and lie face down on the sofa.

"I thought we were headed to the bedroom," he protested.

"We are, but first we relax those muscles you just strained racing me to the house."

Brad chuckled, impressed by her astuteness, as he *had* strained his muscles in the race, although he would never admit it.

He removed his shirt and lay down on the couch, his casted leg dangling off it awkwardly. Shey helped adjust it and lay a pillow underneath to provide more support. "Comfy?"

"Comfortable enough."

"Good." Shey searched through her purse, pulling out a small container of oil. "I always carry some with me because you never know when a little hand action might be needed."

He raised an eyebrow. "Really?"

She giggled. "I wasn't talking about that kind of hand action, Brad."

He chuckled, enjoying the sound of Shey's laughter.

"Now I want you to close your eyes and relax while I work on those muscles." Shey straddled him, being careful not to disturb his leg.

"You know, it still feels as if a gust of wind could blow you away," he commented, noting how light she was. "Have you been eating?"

Shey cleared her throat. "Actually, I didn't have much of an appetite after you left."

"Aww…you missed me that much?"

"No comment," she murmured, pouring the oil all over his back.

He let out a long sigh as her hands began their work, but he couldn't help being intensely aware that her pussy was pressed against his backside as she moved.

She scolded him. "I need you to relax more, mister."

"I'm sorry. There's something about a beautiful redhead straddling my body that gets my libido going."

She giggled again. "Concentrate on my hands and you'll be just fine."

He found her directions amusing because he said something similar to his subs when working them over with his whip.

Brad shut his eyes and gave in to the magic of her expert caress. "I forgot just how talented those hands are."

"Well, I never forgot how sexy your body was," she replied lustfully, kneading the hard muscles of his upper back and shoulders.

His cock grew harder hearing those words, and he turned his head to look up at her. "I think it's time, darlin'."

She licked her lips, her pupils dilating at his suggestion. "I agree."

Shey popped off him after cleaning the remaining oil off her fingers and his back. Handing the crutches to him, she smiled invitingly and quietly followed Brad to the bedroom.

He was surprised, however, when Shey suddenly seemed nervous once she entered his room.

"Nothing to be anxious about," he said in a soothing tone. "This is just a man wanting to express in touch what he cannot say in words."

She looked up, gazing into his eyes and smiled. "I trust you, Brad."

He caressed her cheek, declaring, "And I will never break that trust."

Shey visibly relaxed and nodded.

When Brad had left the redhead in Vegas, he'd felt certain she was the one he was meant to spend his life with, but he hadn't told her that at the time.

Now he would.

Leaning his crutches against the bed, Brad sat down, patting the area beside him. When she took a seat, he cradled her face in his large hand. "I tried so hard to move on, but my mind kept coming back to you and the night we shared."

"Me too."

Brad leaned down, pressing his lips against hers as he

parted them with his tongue to explore her luscious mouth. Breaking away, he took the plunge and confessed, "When I kissed you that last time in Vegas, it felt like I was kissing my soulmate—but you were someone I could never have."

A blush colored her cheeks.

"Do you remember that you said my attraction to Amy was misplaced because I had confused her with the woman I was supposed to fall in love with?"

She giggled softly. "I do."

"You were right. I love you, Shey."

She looked at him in wonder, her eyes filling with tears.

Brad fisted her red hair, pulling Shey's head back to kiss her again. In that moment, he released all the suppressed emotions he had been guarding for so long.

Shey melted into his embrace, stirring things within him he hadn't felt before.

I will not let another man kiss your lips again, he thought.

Tugging at the strap of her dress, he kissed her shoulder and murmured, "Let me love you."

Brad slowly undressed Shey, noting the sprinkling of freckles on her light skin and attempting to kiss every one as he took off her clothes. Once she was completely naked, he asked her to lie on the bed so he could stare at her.

Shey's red hair was fanned out, framing her beautiful face. "You look like the sun itself," he told her. Brad was aroused by the vision before him and unbuttoned his shirt, tossing it onto the nightstand. With some difficulty due to the cast, he removed his socks, pants, and briefs.

His cock was already standing at attention, needing to dive into her warm depths.

He lay on the bed, whipping his casted leg onto it, causing the whole bed to bounce. "Can't wait to get this damn thing off," he muttered, shaking his fist at it.

Brad then looked at Shey and gave her a sexy smirk. "Now, where were we…" He gazed at her feminine body, entranced by the pink hue of her areolas and the darker rose color of her erect nipples.

Growling huskily, he reached out and caressed her breast.

She looked up at him with adoration, pressing herself into his hand to let him know how much she was enjoying the contact. He lowered his head and encased a tempting nipple with his lips, sucking lightly.

Shey's moan sent a jolt through him that traveled straight to his cock.

Everything about her was sexually arousing. Her smell, her taste, her soft skin, and those delectable lips. As much as her body turned him on, it was the over-whelming feeling of love for her that moved him.

With gentle hands and lips, he explored every part of her, entranced by the fact that she loved him too. There was no reason to hold back, no reason to fear rejection anymore.

When she asked to be on top, he willingly lay down, watching with excitement as she slowly lowered herself on his large shaft. He groaned as her wet pussy encased the head of it. Even that would be enough stimulation for him to come, but Shey was a determined woman. She took her time as she rocked against him, taking more and more of his massive cock.

He watched in fascination as that petite frame took the fullness of it. Most women could not take his length no matter how much they desired to, but her body was not only willing but able.

Shey smiled at him, her eyes shining brightly when her mound finally encased the base of his shaft.

"There is nothing sexier than that, darlin'," he stated huskily.

"Except this," she answered as she began moving up and down on his cock.

He grabbed her waist to control her motion, throwing his head back in ecstasy as she caressed his manhood with her femininity.

"Faster," she begged.

He opened his eyes and smirked, taking a tighter grip as he made her dance more vigorously on his cock.

"Yes, yes, oh dear God...yes!" she cried.

He could see the barest outline of his shaft as he moved inside her, and that nearly derailed his control. Slowing down the pace, he pulled her down to him and commanded, "Kiss me."

She moaned as she leaned against his chest and their lips connected. To be fully inside her while he kissed those pink lips was pure heaven. He kept a slow, rhythmic pace, concentrating on the kiss as much as the movement.

"Thrust your tongue in my mouth. I think I'm about to come," Shey begged.

Brad plundered her mouth mercilessly, turned on in the extreme when he felt her body stiffen as her pussy tightened and released around his cock.

"Oh hell, woman!" he groaned, clutching her waist as he increased the pace and gave in to his mounting climax that demanded release. His orgasm was hard and long, burst after burst filling Shey up.

When his climax finally subsided, he released his hold on her and lay back against the pillow, breathing rapidly.

Shey sighed in contentment. "We're good together."

"More than you know, darlin', more than you know..." He ran his fingers through her long red hair, mesmerized by her.

Shey propped her chin on his chest and grinned. "I didn't even notice the cast on your leg."

His chuckle was low when he answered, "Neither did I." He kissed her again before gently rolling her down onto the bed. They stayed connected, her legs wrapped around his as they lay together enjoying the aftereffects of their intense coupling.

The redhead's eyes were closed, her cheeks flushed, and she had a slight smile on her lips.

Brad stared at Shey for a long time, totally captivated by her.

He'd been searching for the right woman for how many years? He actually thought he'd found her when he fell in love with Amy—he was wrong and *never* wanted to feel that kind of pain again.

And yet, he still longed for the depth of love his mother and father shared. As a boy he'd been struck by how much they doted on each other, even though they had been married for years and had a house full of snot-nosed kids.

Brad had since moved on from those simple beginnings in that old Greeley farmhouse, but his parents'
devotion to each other had left a profound imprint. In a
world of continual change, they were a constant.

As he looked down at her, Shey opened her blue eyes
and graced him with a stunning smile. "I love you," she
declared, reaching up to caress his jaw, her eyes sparkling
with tenderness and affection.

He'd waited for this moment all of his life—to have
his love fully returned.

Oh hell, I would do anything for this woman.

Why did the idea of that both excite and terrify him?

Brad needed to sit down with Thane and have a deep
conversation about it. He glanced over at a picture on his
dresser. It was a snapshot of the two of them taken at
the beach during their college days. He was flexing his
pecs while Thane smirked at the camera. It used to make
him smile whenever he looked at it, now it only brought
pain.

Brie is not the only one who needs you, buddy...

Brad Anderson called Tono Nosaka to care for Brie, but he could not have known how difficult it would be for the Kinbaku master. Find out in *Breathe with Me*.

Tono has loved Brie since the very first moment they met at the Submissive Training Center. All he desires is her happiness—she is part of him.

Discover what happens when that love is challenged as we explore the next part of the journey through Tono's eyes.

Buy the next in the series:

#1 (Teach Me)

#2 (Love Me)

#3 (Catch Me)

#4 (Try Me)

#5 (Protect Me)

#6 (Hold Me)

#7 (Surprise Me)

#8 (Trust Me)

#9 (Claim Me)

#10 (Enchant Me)

#11 (A Cowboy's Heart)

#12 (Breathe with Me)

Brie's Submission series:

You can find Red on:
Twitter: @redphoenix69
Website: RedPhoenix69.com
Facebook: RedPhoenix69

**Keep up to date with the newest release of Brie by signing up for Red Phoenix's newsletter:
redphoenix69.com/newsletter-signup**

Red Phoenix is the author of:

Blissfully Undone

* Available in eBook and paperback

(Snowy Fun—Two people find themselves snowbound in a cabin where hidden love can flourish, taking one couple on a sensual journey into ménage à trois)

His Scottish Pet: Dom of the Ages

* Available in eBook and paperback

Audio Book: *His Scottish Pet: Dom of the Ages*

(Scottish Dom—A sexy Dom escapes to Scotland in the late 1400s. He encounters a waif who has the potential to free him from his tragic curse)

The Erotic Love Story of Amy and Troy

* Available in eBook and paperback

(Sexual Adventures—True love reigns, but fate continually throws Troy and Amy into the arms of others)

eBooks

Varick: The Reckoning

(Savory Vampire—A dark, sexy vampire story. The hero navigates the dangerous world he has been thrust into with lusty passion and a pure heart)

Keeper of the Wolf Clan (Keeper of Wolves, #1)

(Sexual Secrets—A virginal werewolf must act as the clan's mysterious Keeper)

The Keeper Finds Her Mate (Keeper of Wolves, #2)

(Second Chances—A young she-wolf must choose between old ties or new beginnings)

The Keeper Unites the Alphas (Keeper of Wolves, #3)

(Serious Consequences—The young she-wolf is captured by the rival clan)

Boxed Set: Keeper of Wolves Series (Books 1-3)

(Surprising Secrets—A secret so shocking it will rock Layla's world. The young she-wolf is put in a position of being able to save her werewolf clan or becoming the reason for its destruction)

Socrates Inspires Cherry to Blossom

(Satisfying Surrender—a mature and curvaceous woman becomes fascinated by an online Dom who has much to teach her)

By the Light of the Scottish Moon

(Saving Love—Two lost souls, the Moon, a werewolf and a death wish…)

In 9 Days

(Sweet Romance—A young girl falls in love with the new student, nicknamed 'the Freak')

---

9 Days and Counting

(Sacrificial Love—The sequel to In 9 Days delves into the emotional reunion of two longtime lovers)

And Then He Saved Me

(Saving Tenderness—When a young girl tries to kill herself, a man of great character intervenes with a love that heals)

Play With Me at Noon

(Seeking Fulfillment—A desperate wife lives out her fantasies by taking five different men in five days)

Connect with Red on Substance B

Substance B is a platform for independent authors to directly connect with their readers. Please visit Red's Substance B page where you can:

- Sign up for Red's newsletter
- Send a message to Red
- See all platforms where Red's books are sold

Visit Substance B today to learn more about your favorite independent authors.

CPSIA information can be obtained
at www.ICGtesting.com
Printed in the USA
LVOW01s1005120317
526915LV00008B/355/P